BAQWA PRESENTS: QUEER CHEER

BAY AREA QUEER WRITERS ASSOCIATION

ANTHOLOGY VOLUME 3

K.S. TRENTEN • PAT HENSHAW

R.L. MERRILL • LIZ FARAIM

RICHARD MAY • VINCENT TRAUGHBER MEIS

M.D. NEU • KELLIANE PARKER

ALLISON FRADKIN • WAYNE GOODMAN

ALEXANDRA CALUEN • ANDREW BEIERLE

SARAH WHITE

ISBN: 978-1-959257-03-5

Design/Layout: Wayne Goodman

waynegoodmanbooks

waynegoodmanbooks@gmail.com
Twitter: @WGoodmanbooks

About BAQWA

The Bay Area Queer Writers Association is a group of local writers who support and encourage each other.

The goal of the group is to create a strong visible writing community here in the San Francisco Bay Area. They are based in Silicon Valley, but they have members from all over the Bay Area.

This group is open to anyone who loves to read and wants to help support area authors. You don't have to live in the Bay Area to be a member, you just have to love Queer books and enjoy reading.

For more information, please visit https://baqwawriters.wixsite.com/books

Table of Contents

Queer Cheer

K.S. Trenten

I wandered the streets, hoping I knew where I was going
Until I came to a door, just a door among many doors.
I knocked upon it, shivering, wondering who might be watching
When a voice murmured through the wood, sending shivers up my spine.

"Are you here for the party?
Are you sure you're at the right one?
You must know what's we're celebrating
If you wish to be welcome."

I hissed, "Queer cheer!"
Heat rising in my cheeks
I wasn't sure how safe I felt saying this
Out in the streets.

The door swung open
A corridor leading to light and laughter
Many a person in costume
Making me feel woefully underdressed.

The smile of my host banished my discomfort
A sweet grin inviting me in on the joke
How elegant they were, a willowy figure in a shimmering sea green gown
Taking my arm as if I was a celebrity.

"Ah, but you are a celebrity!"
They said as if they'd read my thoughts
"I've enjoyed *A Symposium in Space* and *Two*
Not to mention what bubbles in the Cauldron."

My cheeks warmed all the more
Walking at their side amidst the well dressed throng
Two women giggled over glasses of bubbly
The high collars of their old-fashioned gowns undone.

Two men were kissing, hands roaming over each other
Next to a china vase, not under mistletoe
A cluser of flowers sported pansies and hyacinth
Violets, roses, and others I could not name.

I marveled at the diversity of fashion
I'd never seen quite so many hats
Broad-brimmed, feathered, crowned with a ribbon
One woman winked at me under a fedora.

People of various genders leaned against posts in suits
More of a few beyond gender strutted in gowns
Tailored and flowing, ruffled and streamlined
Variety showed itself with flare and elegance.

"Just what are we celebrating?"
I asked while I looked around
"This feels like a special holiday
Only I'm not sure which one it is."

"We're honoring Magnus Hirschfield
For giving the transgendered a home
For offering information and education
For bringing so many people together in his Institute."

"We can't call it St. Magnus Day
There's already a Saint Magnus
We're simply calling it Queer Cheer
Gathering to celebrate it in its various forms."

I glanced at my companion's slight smile
And asked, "What is your name?"
"You can call me Queer Cheer
For my other handles don't matter here."

I glanced at the women in their old-fashioned dresses
The suits in so many different styles
I glanced at a man's face, thinking I'd seen it
In a portrait gallery, painted by an artist long dead.

"Come, you must be thirsty, my scribbler."
Queer Cheer guided me to a punch bowl.
Layers of amber gave way to a richer red
The liquid rippled into cloudy bands of color.

My host poured me a cup
I took a sip, hesitant and shy
Only to taste my first kiss from a woman
Mingled with the honey and fruit.

I sipped the excitement of my first convention
Where others like me had gathered
I'd never known there were so many of us
Finally emerging from our shy internet personas.

I trembled with the joy of when I'd read
The books which spoke to my secret heart
The songs which made me sway and spin
The stories I'd dared to put on a page.

I drank a little of my hopes for the future
The peace and prosperity for which I yearned
The stories trying to explode out of me
Graced with the perfect cover, loved by many.

All of this I tasted with fruit and honey
I gasped, "Just what is in this punch?"
"A little of me and a lot of you.
It's that way for everyone who takes a drink."

Queer Cheer waved their arms to gesture at their guests
"Why do you think the dead come back to this place?
To drink my punch and mingle with each other?
To taste their best and what they hope will come."

Yes, everyone looked giddy as they danced upon the floor
They'd all drunk from the same punch bowl
Queer Cheer took my hand, leading me to the center
"You look like you could use a dance."

"I haven't danced in far too long," I protested
"In that case, you're long overdue."
They took my hands and swayed with me
Letting my foot with its rhythm, matching their grace.

For a time we swayed together
Among couples of every variety
Until Queer Cheer released me and I took another's hand
Couples letting go to form a circle.

We locked our hands and arms together
Letting our hopes and dreams tingle in each other's fingers
We were part of a greater whole, ever expanding
We'd never been alone, no matter how alone we'd felt.

In spite of hate, we could still love
In spite of war, we clutched at moments of peace
In spite of selfishness, we could give
We were greater than any of us could imagine.

I opened my eyes, realized I'd been daydreaming
Swaying to a favorite song
There's no holiday nor person known as Queer Cheer
Except what lives in our hearts, waiting to dance.

Miles to Millicent

Pat Henshaw

"Look, I've been shopping for the perfect gift for months. I need help."

My best friend Fisk leaned out of his front door and gave me a "No shit, Sherlock" squint. He wasn't above trying to make me squirm.

"Let's see. This would be for Miles, right?" He had a teasing gleam in his eyes. "For Valentine's Day? Yes?"

I nodded and opened my mouth to speak. Fisk ignored my attempt at discussion.

"This would be a gift for the same Miles you've been living with for three years and dating for an extra two before he moved in, Zack?"

"Yes, but you don't–"

He cut me off before I could finish my sentence. He had a point, but as usual, whatever the point was, it missed me by a mile. He held both hands up, palms out.

"If you, who know him much better than I, can't think of the perfect gift, why ask me to pull your ass out of the hopper?"

"No. Stop. Wait. You don't understand." I quickly jumped in, interrupting him.

Everyone knew I was an uninspired gift-giver. I mostly relied on ties, shirts, and sometimes socks.

"I know what I want to give him. I just don't know where to get it. The places I've tried haven't been very helpful. I'm running out of time." I hated to admit it, especially to Fisk.

"You need my shopping prowess and my unerring mojo." He was all but rubbing his hands together as he purred in satisfaction. "Well, why didn't you say? Or at least grovel?"

I bowed slightly, a grin on my lips. "I kneel at your feet, O Fairy of Dreams Come True."

He pulled me inside his condo, brushed aside the hanging beads, and tugged me into his kitchen where he'd built what his husband Grady called a Shrine to Coffee. The coffee-shop-worthy monster gleamed its silver smile at me.

"Sit, sit." Fisk told me with a push toward a chair and turned to fiddle with the machine. "Now tell me all."

"First, before I give you my shopping list, you have to promise not to tell Grady or Miles. You can't even hint at it to Miles. And if you tell Grady right now…" I was bent over the table glaring at Fisk.

"If I tell Grady, the love of my life and the spark who keeps me going… well," he sighed. "Well, Grady will inadvertently tell one of his jabber-mouthed friends who will spread it far and wide." He sighed again.

With a dainty pinch of his pointer finger and thumb, he mimed zipping his lips together.

"Consider me silenced."

"Don't worry. I'll tell him at the last minute, well, the last couple hours. I'll need his help too."

The monster belched, providing us with two perfect coffee drinks.

"Now tell me all."

Fisk assured me the only–the ONLY–place to shop to get everything on my list for Miles was the Emporium.

The Emporium started as an area munitions dump and motor pool during World War II. A state-of-the-art cinder block and steel reinforced rectangle the size of four football fields placed side by side, it hulked in the South Bay like an ever-vigilant toad. The stark building was surrounded by pavement for parking huge pieces of equipment and the hundreds of cars of the workers.

A ghost of the war era, the former ammo dump remained vacant for years. Just as it was being considered for destruction, an entrepreneur bought it, cleaned up one end, and opened a garage sale area for rent by those without garages. Slowly, the Emporium was born.

Walking past its open barn-like doors felt like a sensual assault. Bright colors and flashing lights fought with the cacophony of haggling voices and blaring music from the far corners of the world. The air ran wild with perfumes, spices, and manure from the sales tables and the animal auction.

"Fasten your seat belt," Miles had cautioned the first time we'd visited the Emporium, "'cuz it might be a bumpy ride."

We'd held hands–the only way not to get separated from someone in the crowd–and we'd faced the Emporium together.

This time although I was with Fisk, there was no way I was holding his hand. I might as well have been on my own.

As we stepped into the maelstrom, a tall rotund man waddled up to us.

"Fisk! Fisk! Fisk, my friend!" Like a human Tyrannosaurus rex, he extended a short arm ending in a long-nailed hand. The nails, painted blood red, reached toward us in greeting.

Fisk bypassed the hand and nails, pushing in to give the rex a hug.

"Cosmo! Your Emporium looks and smells and sounds like a dream come true. Well done. Well done."

Cosmo preened for a moment, pulling back his talons and standing proud.

"So, what can I help you find, you and your beautiful friend?" The huge man eyed me like I was a piece of veal ready to be sold in one of the stalls.

I'm five feet eight inches tall, with porcelain skin, intense blue eyes, and yellow-gold hair. I've been asked if I was Swedish, Danish, Finnish, or elf. Cosmo looked ready to gobble me up. I stood taller, hoping to channel my inner Viking warrior.

Fisk, as usual, missed my being uneasy and jumped right in.

"Ah, this is Zack, a do-gooder lawyer who needs to find the perfect Valentine's Day gift for his tall, dark, and handsome lover."

I smiled, but didn't extend my hand, nor did Cosmo offer me his. With Fisk's introduction, the lines had been drawn, and I was free to shop.

Cosmo gave me a lingering look and a sigh, then brightened.

"My lovely Zack, you have come to exactly the right place." He turned and waved his hand toward the hubbub. "Here, you can get anything you want."

I swallowed a laugh. Was he quoting the lyrics to Arlo Guthrie's Alice's Restaurant? Should I reply, "Excepting Alice"?

Fisk elbowed me and gave a tiny shake of his head. His gesture shouted, "Don't poke the bear!" Or maybe he was saying I needed to be fenced in?

He turned to the rex-armed grizzly.

"Cosmo, Zack is feeling a little overloaded amid the lushness. Is there a buyer room available so I can shop for him and let him select his purchases without being too caught up in the fun?"

Cosmo laughed, a sound which stopped the surrounding buyers and sellers for a moment.

"In other words, you think you can find what he wants better than he can?" Cosmo's eyes twinkled toward Fisk, then he turned to survey me from top to bottom again. "You're probably right. You're probably right."

I started to protest. I opened my mouth and got another poke in the ribs from Fisk.

"Thank you, Cosmo. We appreciate your accommodation."

With a shake of my head, I followed the beacon called Cosmo to a curtained off stall space. He pulled back the fabric from the middle of the drape and gestured for us to enter.

I guessed this was a usual stall size space, but it had been curtained off on all four sides. The empty room held two card tables side-by-side across from the entrance. Two folding chairs were stationed under tables. On the top of one table was a scattering of cocktail napkins, a pen, and a couple of sheets of paper. The floor was scuffed as if groups of people had recently come and gone.

Cosmo gave the space a quick glance and sighed.

"Your friend Zack drinks tea, yes?" Without waiting for an answer, Cosmo turned and lifted the tent flap. "I will order tea," he yelled over his shoulder, sailing through the space and letting the flap drop.

Fisk and I looked at each other, shrugged, and laughed.

"A warning, Zack. Don't drink the tea. I think they make it from manure."

Fisk left at the same time my phone buzzed. Miles. Now what?

"Hey, big M. What's up?" I tried to sound as normal and unflustered as possible. The ambient madhouse sounds outside the open-topped tent seemed to grow louder.

"Where the hell are you, Zack? Has there been an accident? Are you okay?" Miles was an unflappable defense attorney who only lost it when I got myself in a mess.

"Chill, Miles. I'm fine." I took a deep breath and confessed. "I'm with Fisk at the Emporium."

I could feel him getting miffed. The silence was tense and growing even more deafening.

"Now what has he talked you into?" Occasionally, Miles wasn't Fisk's greatest fan.

"Nothing. We just wanted to check it out. How are things at the office?"

Miles hated when I changed the subject, especially when he wanted details. But sometimes he played along. This was sometime.

"Fine. Everything's fine here. Enjoy your day off. I called to say I might be a little late. I'll know more in a couple of hours." He sounded harried. "Don't let Fisk talk you into one of his stupid ideas. You don't need to save him."

Fisk did not talk me into anything stupid. Instead, he helped me find exactly what I wanted to give Miles for Valentine's Day.

Saturday, February 14, began inauspiciously. Miles had to go into the office for a half day.

"Sometimes I think you're the smarter one, Zack. Pro bono only seems to happen during the week days," he grumbled as I straightened his tie.

I gave him my brilliant smile and nodded.

"Happy Valentine's Day. Remember we're going out to dinner tonight and you need to be here to freshen up before we leave."

"Yes, dear." He sounded like a pouty six-year-old, but the twinkle in his eyes said he was way, way past puberty. "I got you a little something."

Miles wasn't a heavy-handed gift kind of guy, so his admission came out shyly as if I'd turn down a gift from him.

"And I have a little something for you." I straightened his tie and gave it a playful tug. "Now go play with the other attorneys. Don't let anyone overrule you."

"I'd rather be playing with you," he grumbled after giving me a kiss.

He left. Fisk called to say he'd told Grady about the surprise and they were primed to come over and help me get ready whenever I needed them. I laughed, thanked him, and spent the rest of the day worrying if Miles would like my gift.

At seven, a tired, rumpled, drooping Miles got home.

"Honey, how about if we get take out? I'm bushed." He sounded even worse than he looked.

"Oh, uh, well, in that case, don't go into the bedroom. I got all your clothes ready for you to go out." I was in shirt, tie, and dress pants. I tried not to look as disappointed as I felt. I really had tried to get this gift right.

Miles stared at me a few moments, then sighed. He took a deep breath and smiled.

"Okay, let's do it. Good food. Relaxing atmosphere. The most handsome, loveable man in the universe by my side. Then we can come home and kick back… and kick back." His smile was tired but game.

Now, I was really nervous. What if he didn't like my present? As we walked to the bedroom door which I'd closed after getting his gift ready, I almost stopped and told him we'd stay home. No problem.

Still, he had told me my present was something he dreamed about, so there was no turning back.

I slowly pushed the door open.

Miles stopped and stared.

On the bed was a gold lamé gown, matching long gloves, a clutch purse, fishnet hose, a garter belt and matching panties. On the floor were a pair of gold heels.

Miles hadn't made a sound, so I turned and looked at him.

Tall, dark, handsome, barracuda defense attorney Miles, who chews up prosecutors and their witnesses with hardly a snarl, had tears in his eyes. I opened my mouth, but no sound came out.

Suddenly he grabbed me and hugged me so hard I thought I might stop breathing.

"Zack..." He gulped back a sob. "Zack, thank you. Thank you. I love you so much."

Then he pushed me away but kept his hands on my upper arms.

"You want me to put it on now? I can wear it to dinner tonight? You're sure? You won't mind being seen with me?" His eyes were searching my face. For what, I had no clue.

"Of course. I just hope it all fits." Then I started to worry. "You do want to wear it? To dinner at the Grotto tonight? Right? Or do you want to think about it for–"

"Absolutely not. Are you crazy?" He wiped away the moisture from his eyes. "After my mother saw me try on her heels when I was nine, she said if any girl knew about me, no one would ever love me, and I'd always be alone. Then when I came out, she told me I was unlovable, a disgrace, and God would punish me. I tried to reform. Really. I tried to stop wanting..." His hand waved toward the bed.

Now it was my turn to wipe his tears.

"I hope you know your mother was completely wrong. You are loved. By me, by your friends, by our friends, the clients you help. But mostly by me. And right now, you're wasting time." I gave him a kiss. "Grady is coming over in a few minutes to do your makeup, and you know how he doesn't like waiting around."

Grady was a professional film makeup artist, and, as he kept telling everyone, he had the awards to prove it.

"Grady's coming over? To do my makeup?" Miles had straightened and looked suitably awed at the prospect. "Better get ready then."

I'd undone his tie and unbuttoned his shirt in between kisses and hugs. Now I started on his pants.

"No time to waste, sweetie. Hop to it."

When he slipped on the silk panties, he started getting frisky.

"Not now, big guy. We have lots of time after dinner."

He sighed but got himself under control so we could wrestle with the garter belt and hose. The fishnet hose proved to be a challenge, first from his sticking his toes through the holes, then trying to push down the hair on his legs. We gave up on the hair, and he slithered into the dress.

"You look magnificent, Miles."

He was standing at the full-length mirror as if caught up in rapture.

"Milly," he murmured. "I'm not Miles. I'm Milly."

I gasped.

"No, you're not. Absolutely not."

He looked at me, devastation and horror crumpling his face.

"What? You don't—"

"Milly is a silly miss who simpers and gives everyone big, innocent eyes," I told him with a shake of my head. "You are Miss Millicent, tall, statuesque, austere, above all the rest of us common folk. You are a goddess, a person we can only bow to and grovel at your feet. You are so much better than silly Milly." I gave him a wink. "I'm shocked you can even suggest such a name."

During my harangue, he had turned to the mirror and transformed as I watched. His shoulders went back, his chin went up, and his mouth settled on a sly Mona Lisa smile.

"You're right, Zack. I'm not Milly. I was never Milly."

I picked up his long gold lame gloves. Grady was knocking at the front door.

"Here put these on while I let Grady in."

Like an EMT arriving at the scene of an accident, Grady carried two huge tackle boxes. His pinkie finger held the strings of a hat box.

"You didn't leave me much time, Zack," he grumbled as he marched to the bedroom.

I followed after him.

"Thanks for–"

I halted and nearly ran into Grady who was staring at Miles.

"Not bad," Grady said. "Turn around."

A scared-looking, wide-eyed Miles slowly rotated.

"Not bad at all. I can work with this." Grady turned and his boxes banged into me. "To the kitchen, we haven't a moment to lose."

I stood aside, letting him push past me.

Miles sat down on the side of the bed and tried to put on his heels. His gloves were rumpled, hindering his progress.

I knelt in front of him and slipped on his shoes. Then I stood and smoothed the wrinkles on his gloves. I helped him stand.

"Well, Cinderella, are you ready for the next step in getting ready for the ball?"

He gave me a Miss Millicent spiked eyebrow and a conspiratorial grin.

"Ball? I'm not going to the ball. There's no point. I already have the prince."

With that he sailed out of the room, only tripping a little on his way to the kitchen.

To say Geppetto's Grotto of Truth Bistro was packed would be an understatement. Valentine's Day had brought out everyone, queer, and straight alike. Since Geppetto's is a family owned and run restaurant, everyone was a friend or neighbor. We had all tacitly agreed early on that we wouldn't post glowing reviews on social media but keep the restaurant as our own hidden gem. Still, there were more people than double the tables. No one was angry about this, but seemed to be waiting for takeout or reservation spaces as if they were at a reunion.

I helped Miles up to the door, propping him up as he stumbled across the gravel parking lot.

We parked in the staff area like Marty told us to. As the grandson of the owner, Marty deferred to Gramma Ava, who now in her nineties ran the daily operation from her throne on the balcony looking down at the diners. Marty said Gramma Ava wanted to see us walk in. She knew something big was going to happen.

Millicent took a moment to get herself together before we entered the foyer. Couples nodded to me and looked puzzled at Millicent as we made our way over the pebbles. One woman said, "Careful, dear. The parking lot is treacherous." She wasn't talking to me. Millicent had nodded with a quiet, but confident, "Thank you."

Finally ready to make her grand entrance, Millicent took my arm, shook her shoulders, and lifted her chin. She looked and acted every inch a queen.

Music from a Putumayo recording blared from the speakers giving Geppetto's an international feel. Everyone standing around in the foyer had left the door area free and clear enough that Millicent and I had no trouble making an entrance. Being six foot five and usually commanding attention, she immediately caught everyone's eye.

Marty hustled up to us, his hands pointing up at Gramma Ava.

"Bellissima!" she bellowed, raising her frail hands to clap.

Millicent and I bowed to her and waved.

Gramma Ava bowed back and gestured for us to be on our way to our table.

Marty seated us by the window overlooking the vegetable and herb garden, a prime spot. We weren't given menus, but one of Gramma's great-grandchildren or maybe a great-great-grandchild served us glasses of Pellegrino.

"Enjoy," he whispered.

Gramma Ava shouted down to him, "Speak up, boy! Nobody can hear you."

He looked up at her in surprise and fled.

"We aren't ordering?" Millicent asked.

I shook my head.

"Marty said he would surprise us."

Millicent nodded and took a sip of water.

"In that case, while we wait for our meal, I'd like to, um, give you, um, something."

Millicent scrabbled around in her evening bag for a few seconds while people talked in hushed voices around us. I caught a few of the comments, and gathered they were wondering who Zack was out to dinner with on Valentine's Day. No one had made the connection to Miles yet. How unobservant of them.

Millicent stood and clumsily got down on one knee. She cleared her throat.

"Um, Zack, my love, will you make me the happiest man on earth and marry me?"

A gasp reverberated around us.

It took me a few seconds. Then his words hit me. Happiness bubbled up around us. I was so happy I could have been standing in an empty chamber with only the two of us.

We both had been planning what the other had longed for.

"Of course! Yes! Of course." I didn't know whether I should stand and help Millicent up or get down on my knees with her… him.

Millicent put a ring on my finger. Then tried to stand but caught her dress.

"Dammit, now I'm going to cry," she said as I jumped up to help her. Her face crumpled, and she started sobbing.

I handed her my handkerchief–something I'd brought along for the occasion in case Miles got teary. She cried louder.

"What's wrong?" I was starting to panic. What had I done now?

People were milling around us asking each other what was happening as the wait staff tried to get eat-in customers seated and orders taken, and carryout handed to take-out customers. The noise level nearly drowned out Millicent's answer.

But standing so close to him in my little bubble made it easy to hear his voice.

"I love you so much, Zack. I always dreamed of being dressed in something like this and asking the man of my dreams to marry me. You made it all happen." She used my hankie to mop up, a lot of Grady's hard work coming off in the process.

I was stunned.

I'd done it?

I'd given the glorious, magnetic, handsome Miles a present that turned out to be perfect? As I looked down at the ring he'd given me, I knew I'd never be able to give him such a gift again. I was just happy I could do it once.

Let Me Stand Next to Your Fire

R.L. Merrill

Act One

She sits on a lounge chair in front of the bright orange glow. Watching the reflection of the flames in her eyes is like viewing an old twenty-millimeter film as it flickers and dances. I've often said that she could never be more picturesque than at this very moment and been proven wrong time and again. She's swimming in an old wool sweater with a giant cowl neck, and as I watch the soft material brush against her neck as she talks, I swear I'm going to combust.

Lena is my best friend.

She is the most beautiful woman I've ever seen.

And I'm hopelessly in love with her, and she doesn't have a clue.

I slide my chair a little closer to take advantage of the hand she has dangling, palm up, extended from the armrest. She might be trying to make a point in our conversation, but I can't draw my eyes away from her, nor cease my internal debate over whether or not her hand's position is a potential invitation.

"All I'm saying is maybe we should just go." She smooths her satiny black hair with her other hand and then stretches her pink sweatpants-clad legs out, her bare feet illuminated by the fire. Her outfit doesn't match in any sort of way, but then she doesn't care. Lena wears what's comfortable. Period. She had a pedicure today and hasn't chipped it yet, which she'll consider a win. I've never seen anything as touchable as her toes.

"Things are so crazy at my company. You hate your job," she continues. "We could be like that one movie where the women run away together."

"*Thelma and Louise?* You haven't killed anyone lately, have you?" I always distract her with humor when she talks like this.

Doing a geographic sound nice, but we've always been realists. We make plans and stick to them. We've always been the room moms and the sports team volunteers for the kids. We were dutiful wives and mothers, and now it's just us. Although, I have to admit what she's describing sounds like a dream come true.

"What are you talking about?" She turns, and the curve of her bottom lip glistens in the firelight. Maybe she's just taken a sip of her water. Maybe she ran her lovely pink tongue over it.

Here, in the darkness, I can stare a bit more freely than I normally would. I fantasize about those lips. I've watched them move for years, but how would they feel? What would she say if I pressed my own against them?

"Remember? They went on the run because one of them killed her mans."

And then she laughs.

It slays me.

She inhales, and as she forces sound from her lovely chest, it creates the spark that sets off the wildfire inside of me. The flames catch every flammable substance in their path until they are consumed and the fire, like me, is desperate for more oxygen.

"That's right. I haven't killed anyone, sorry. Can we still go?"

She rests her chin on her right shoulder and looks up at me with those soulful brown eyes as dark as this March night. It's the Spring Equinox, the start of a new season, and I can't help but wonder if maybe...

Could there be a start of something new for us, too?

I want to give her everything she asks for. I can't maintain this charade any longer. I can't breathe.

The fingers on her inviting hand twitch again, and I'm helpless.

I know her hands are warm and soft, so soft. She's touched me with those fingers many times before. Braided my hair when it was longer, applied my makeup with a steadier hand than I ever could, and zipped up a stubborn dress while protecting my delicate skin with her hand on my back. Those actions, so innocent, and yet they've fueled my wonderings for all this time. Does she know how my ridiculous heart has held onto those moments? How those brushes with intimacy fed my soul for so many years?

How do I tell her I've longed for her for what feels like a lifetime? Since we had drama together in seventh grade? Since we got drunk on the elementary school playground in the dead of night as teenagers and avoided getting caught? Spent hours fighting over unworthy boys? Since we cried over the phone while thousands of miles away in college? And after moving back to our hometown with our husbands, we raised our children as neighbors…

All of this adds up to the realization that I've been in love with Lena since we were thirteen years old. Back then, I thought the intensity of my love for her was because she was my best friend. She'd stood by my side when everyone else laughed at my latest clumsy move, lack of social graces, and absent fashion sense. I was a hopeless mess facing a world of unforgiving peers while struggling with my mother's mental illness, but Lena never cared about trivial shit. She cared about me. In return for her loyal friendship, I listened to hours of tearful protests over her issues with her parents. They weren't happy with her "life choices." At thirteen. Who makes life choices at thirteen? We made "the next five minutes" choices at that age. When we became parents and our own kids hit that age, we totally laughed at how ridiculous we'd been back then and how unrealistic our parents were.

Lena has been my "ride or die" since then. But somewhere along the way, I realized that the hours we spent lightly scratching each other's backs in bed on countless sleepovers was more than just soothing each other. For me, at least. I'd memorized the topography of her body; the cut of her shoulder blades, the slight curve of her spine from scoliosis, and the scars from the acne she tried so hard to hide that made her self-conscious but were perfect in my eyes. Every bit of her was beautiful to me and, I touched her with as much reverence now as I did then.

She'd figured out that she was queer before I even had a clue about myself. *Always the late bloomer, Dani.* After her cheating husband left her, she opened herself to all possibilities and dated frequently. Watching her live her life out loud and seeing her kids root her on pushed me toward my own realization.

I loved my husband Tucker desperately and still mourned his death from cancer two years ago when we were both forty-five. It was so unfair. Our kids had just finished high school. We should have had more time together. We had plans.

Lena loved him, too. They were football buddies, shouting at the TV in tandem while I chased the kids around them. They ogled women together when the three of us went out for dinner and fought over which one of them would have the best chance at scoring. When he died, Lena held me through my tears and helped me take care of the business of being a widow. Along the way, I had an epiphany.

I'd absolutely loved Tucker with my whole being. I was sexually attracted to him. He was my best friend.

And I felt the same way about Lena, even though we'd never crossed that line of intimacy.

Oh, how I want to cross it.

Now that we're fading into middle age, our bodies have begun withering subtly with each passing day. Lena had a breast cancer scare last year and is under a doctor's care for brutal arthritis. I'm looking at a medically necessary hysterectomy soon. We watch our children live their lives to extremes, usually making good decisions like we taught them. Life choices. My Casey married his sweetheart right out of college, and my Beth shares a house with Lena's Andre and Arabella while the three of them navigate graduate school and big, important careers. Lena and I talk all the time about how proud we are of what they've accomplished and pat each other on the back for being great moms.

But what now? I work for the corporate offices of a grocery chain and write cozy mysteries on the side. Lena's a CPA and dreams of running a bustling tax business out of her home that will keep her comfortable throughout the year. Do we keep doing these things until we can't anymore and then die? In separate households mere doors away from each other? Or could we actually run away? Live a different kind of life in a different sort of relationship?

I wish for the rest of our days to be spent wrapped around each other like a warm sweater, protecting us from the harsh realities of aging. I want all of our nights to be like this one. The two of us gazing at the sparks from the fire traveling from the flames in the metal pit up toward the sky to dance with the stars.

I finally take the bait and slide my fingers against her palm, lacing them with hers. It's not that unusual for us to hold hands. It's the safest way for me to pretend we're more than lifelong friends.

"We *could* run away," I say, afraid to sound too hopeful. "Or we could just stay right here by the fire."

My heart throbs as the minutes pass, and she doesn't move her hand. She merely breathes in and out, her chest rising and falling, a thoughtful smile playing on those lips.

"It *is* a beautiful night. And I love the fire."

I love you.

I wish I could say the words and she would understand.

"Yeah. I'm digging this fire pit," I say instead. "All we need is marshmallows and some sticks."

"I don't need anything else," she says. And then she squeezes my hand.

*I don't need any*one *else.*

I wonder how much longer I can keep holding her hand before she pulls it away. What is the appropriate amount of time for a friendly clasp of hands? Is it just until the other acknowledges their affection with a slight squeeze? Then do you count to three and let go?

Or is it go on three?

A chuckle slips out as I think of the ridiculous scene from *Lethal Weapon,* and I use the distraction to let go, but as our fingers slide apart, she fumbles. She grasps for mine in a firmer hold. Then adds a second hand, which means she's now facing me.

"Can I say something?"

"You can say anything."

She hates it when I answer like that. It's usually followed by the juvenile *"it's a free country."*

But this time I don't respond like a brat. I've been feeling a sense of urgency lately, and it makes me bold, so when she rolls her eyes, I answer, "I'm listening."

She exhales as though she's about to make a confession. I know this as I've been on the receiving end so many times. Her deepest darkest secrets, fears, loves, joys… And I've rewarded her by keeping a big secret from her.

How's that for a shitty best friend? I often wonder if she would view my omission as a betrayal. Keeping my true feelings from her could be a mistake. But the consequences would be too much for me to take if she doesn't reciprocate.

"Okay, I don't really want to run away, but I want… that. Like, the two of us, together, taking on the world, having adventures. It's always been you and me. I want it that way."

She groans as the words leave her mouth, and I start dancing in my chair and singing, doing my best Backstreet Boys impression.

"I'm sorry," I say, trying to get myself together. The giggles have taken over in a desperate plea to ease the tension in this conversation.

A loud pop from the fire scares us both, and then she's laughing with me. As the hiccups set in, we lay back and gaze at the stars until our breathing is normal again.

And she reaches for my hand, which I'd left palm up, dangling from the armrest.

I think I'm feverish. Did she mean it? Was she saying what I've so desperately wanted to say to *her* for many moonlit starry nights over the decades?

She squeezes gently.

"We could go on quoting silly songs and making movie references all night, or I could quote your stupid favorite line from that stupid testosterone-laden fighter pilot movie."

My mouth runs dry… "Maverick, you big stud?"

She nods slowly. "Take me to bed–"

"Or lose you forever?"

Those lips slide into that smile of hers that always results in her getting her way. The one that she used several hours ago to get me to agree to cook tonight, and to pick up the Ben & Jerry's, and to make her a fire in the backyard.

"Yes. No. I mean the middle part."

"Are you tired?"

She drops my hand and sighs.

I fear I've snuffed the fire out, sucked the necessary oxygen from it in my desperate attempt to protect my heart.

"Dani, are you really going to keep up these evasive maneuvers?"

"I… evasive?"

"You'll joke to get out of dealing with anything. Don't joke with me. Be honest with me."

"What are you asking me?" I turn to face her and fight back the panic threatening to suffocate me.

"Have you ever thought about us?"

I open my mouth fully intending to continue playing dumb. She deserves better than that.

"You mean being intimate?"

She smiles at me and blinks several times. I notice she took off her makeup before coming over. She looks so much like the Lena from high school. Maybe her face is slimmer, more angular, but she's my Lena. I know I can tell her anything, and she'll take it and keep it. She'll protect it. She'll respect it.

"I know you haven't been with a woman," she says, "but you told me once that you thought about it."

I *had* told her that. One night after she'd been on a date she'd come over and we sat outside just like this, minus the fire pit. She told me everything. How different it was having a woman pleasure her, how weird it felt to be the one playing with boobs, and we'd laughed for hours. I can't believe she remembers my confession.

I want to experience that someday.

What I'd left out was that I wanted it to be *her*.

"Are you serious, Lena? Don't play with me."

She rests her elbow on the arm of her chair and grins wickedly.

My heart goes from zero to eighty-five in less than a second.

"Yeah. I want to play with you, but I'm not playing. Come on. Tell me you never thought about us, and I won't bring it up again."

I don't answer her right away. I can't even look at her. I'm terrified. Will she understand how I feel? My hesitation is only because… what if? What if

I'm a bad kisser? What if she doesn't find me attractive like that? What if I lose the most important person in my life?

I can't look at her. "I've thought about it. For a long time."

My admission is out there. I can never take it back. It will hang between us no matter what happens next.

"Da-ni." She gives my name the singsong treatment, trying to get me to look at her, and I laugh. I can't ignore her. Ever. She'll pester me, poke me in the arm, pull my hair, whatever it takes to get me to look at her.

Her smile is full of mischief and promise. And yet…

"What about the last part of that line? That's my biggest fear."

She shakes her head. "You're never getting rid of me."

She stands from the lounge chair and pulls me to my feet. Nearly the same height, roughly the same build, definitely both nervous, our hands tremble as we embrace.

This is different from hugging her.

Our hugs have always been full-bodied, bordering on wrestling moves meant to subdue an opponent. One of us would lift the other off our feet, we'd rock back and forth, and the world would always be right.

Tonight we are drawn to each other, and I make a point to pay attention to every point of contact. Our arms brush first, and then our chests meet next. The rest of our torsos press together–her's fit, mine soft–and our thighs connect. But it's her face, so close to mine, that is my undoing. I rest my forehead on her shoulder and I shudder, letting the air out of my lungs so I can feel her even closer to me.

"I've waited forever for you." My eyes burn. "I would have continued waiting forever."

Her lips graze my ear. "I was afraid you would *take* forever."

She forces me to look at her, and the excitement flickers in her eyes like the flames dancing beside us.

"I want forever. With you. I want so much."

I brush her hair back from her face, to be certain, to stare into her familiar eyes and see the truth there. My thumbs caress her cheeks, and I let one drift toward those beckoning lips I'm longing for.

"What do you want?" I ask, though I'm getting the hint. She's already slid her hands inside the waistband of my yoga pants and up my back to unfasten my bra.

"Let me stand next to your fire," she whispers and she takes my thumb into her mouth, biting down just enough to weaken my knees.

My nerves never cease to bring out the songstress in me, and I whisper-sing the Hendrix lyrics.

She silences me with her kiss and my world burns.

Flames consume us both as I finally kiss her and I'm surprised that it's not awkward. There's no unease. It's just like kissing Tucker, but not. I feel the same warmth fueled by trust, familiarity, and love. I'm vulnerable before her, but she kisses me, and I'm not afraid. It's her but it's *not* her. I'm kissing Lena, but it's a *new* Lena that I have yet to experience, and she's scorching.

"You taste good, like warm honey," she says. "Let's go inside."

"*Inside* inside? Like the bedroom? Lena–"

"I promise we'll only do what you're comfortable with."

A laugh escapes. "I'm not *comfortable* with anything."

She pulls back but I hold her in place.

"Dani?"

"No, wait. This isn't comfortable," I say and my voice lowers.

Now that she's in my arms, it's like the volcano has erupted, and lava flows freely down the mountainside, scorching everything in its path, clearing away the doubts that had cropped up like tiny seedlings since the last eruption.

"This is what it feels like to watch pyrotechnics. It's terrifying and thrilling at the same time, but not comfortable." I slide my hands down her sides and grip her hips tightly. "Front row at Metallica, remember? The fire nearly scorched your fake eyelashes off and my face was red for days afterward. It was a rush. That's what I mean."

Lena runs her hands up my ribcage and her thumbs graze my breasts. I want more than a graze. I want her to really touch me.

"If you want a rush, take me to bed."

Instead of finishing the quote, I kiss her once more. For luck. For bravery. For reassurance.

She's my Lena and she loves me. Whatever happens when we go inside, she'll always be mine.

"What about the fire?" I ask, always the responsible one. I don't want to be responsible for the neighborhood burning down.

She pulls away and shovels sand over the embers, and then places the cover over it.

It's so dark outside I can't see her face as she approaches me.

"Get your ass inside before we explode," she says as she passes me and I am done making jokes. I come after her and she squeals as I chase her through my dark house. I'm a fireball hurtling through space and she's my target. She stops at my bedside and places her hands on my cheeks. "You're so hot, Dani. Come keep me warm."

"Burn, baby, burn."

Act Two

I wake up to banging noises and a suffocating feeling I can't ignore.

I suck in a big breath of air and realize my mistake. I'm drowning.

"Are you okay?"

It's Lena.

Well, it's Lena's hair. In my face. Over my face, actually, and probably in my lungs now.

She flicks her mane back and pushes up onto her knees. I cough a few times and she looks worried. Then I grin.

"Good morning."

Her smile is brighter than the sun coming through my bedroom window since I left the drapes open. We'd been in a bit of a hurry last night.

My smile is goofier than, I don't even know. I'm plumb out of descriptive language this morning.

"Hi."

Wow. Apparently I'm out of most words in the English language.

Lena laughs and straddles my waist.

"Hi."

She's fucking gorgeous and she's all mine. Finally.

The fact that she kisses me again, pre-toothbrushing, leads me to think she enjoyed last night as much as I did.

The fact that she's still naked and kissing her way down my neck, to my breasts, to below that–

"Oh. God. *Lena.*"

Just as I'm able to relax–I'd had the same problem last night–and I'm losing myself in the rhythm of her tongue, I hear banging again.

"What the–"

I hear laughter. Familiar laughter. Feminine familiar laughter.

Oh God.

"Lena."

"Mom?"

Lena stops her, um, activity.

I pull the sheet over her.

Beth knocks on the door twice and comes in without waiting for an answer.

I smile innocently.

"Did I wake you?" Beth asks, confusion on her face.

Lena snorts.

Beth stops just as she's about to plop onto the bed.

We stare at each other.

"Hi," I say, which makes Lena laugh again.

"Mom?"

"Yes?"

Oh. Good. I apparently know another word.

"Did you… is that… am I?"

Lena pulls the sheet off her head, her hair wild, and tucks it around herself as she curls up next to me.

"Yes, we forgot you guys were coming over," she says. "Yes, it's me. And yes, you're interrupting."

I still have the same innocent smile on my face. It's kind of frozen there now, and my cheeks are starting to hurt. If I try to speak, my face will probably crack.

"Hi." I say again, and this time Lena loses it.

"What's going–Mom?"

Andre and Arabella come in behind Beth and now there are three pairs of puzzled eyes peering down at us, astounded.

"Hi." Lena gives her kids a little finger wave and they look at each other.

"Mom, did you forget we were coming for breakfast?" Beth appears to be most preoccupied with the lack of food prepared rather than the fact that she just walked in on her mother having sex with the woman she's considered an aunt her entire life. *That's my girl. Food first.*

"I... maybe? We, um–"

"We were up late last night, so we decided to sleep in." Lena replies matter-of-factly.

"When she says last night, she really means this morning," I say, taking Lena's hand and lacing our fingers together on top of the sheets. "What was it, four? When we finally went to sleep?"

"Mmm hmmm, yep. Four sounds about right. Anyhoo, all the fixins are in the fridge because Dani went to the store yesterday and she cooked me dinner–"

"And I bought you Ben & Jerry's, which was delicious. Good call by the way."

"It *was* a good call. You're welcome."

Lena leans over and kisses me and I'm just so damn happy I could care less that our kids might be about to stroke out over what they just walked in on.

Lena turns with eyebrows raised and looks at Arabella. "You guys can get started on the food and we'll be out in a jiffy. Kay?"

The three kids nod, look at each other with their heads tilted to the side, brows furrowed, and they file out of the room, closing the door behind them.

And we burst out laughing.

"I really did forget," I say, surprised at myself.

"I didn't," Lena said. "We always do brunch with them on the first Saturday of the month."

I snap my fingers. "That's right! Wow. I never forget."

Lena squeezes my hand. "See how easy that was?"

One of the conversations we'd had late into the night had been about how the hell we were going to tell the kids about our change in status.

"For all they know, this could have been going on for a long time," Lena had said with a shrug. The sheet had been draped around her waist, and I'd been a little mesmerized by her swaying breasts, not gonna lie. I'd spent so many years trying not to gaze fondly upon them and now that they were mine to ogle, I quickly lost all focus.

"I guess it could have been."

Lena had scolded me for not talking to her sooner. "I always thought maybe," she'd said. "But I never wanted to push you. I know how much you love Tucker."

"Somehow I think Tucker would be quite pleased with how things turned out," I said to her, shaking my head. "He suggested once that we invite you to move in with us, after what's-his-name left."

"What's-his-name," she said, rolling her eyes. "That might have been fun, but I don't think, as much as Tucker liked to goof off with me, that he would have shared you with anyone."

That was when I'd cried. And just like all the other times I'd needed her, Lena had held me through it all.

"I kept waiting for you to date someone, anyone," she'd said. "Then I would know you were ready. But you're so..."

"Clueless? Stubborn? Lame?"

She'd shushed me and kissed my tears away. "No, silly. You needed time. I wanted to give it to you, but it's been hard."

"Thank you," I'd whispered, snuggling up against her. Our legs were entwined, and she kept tickling me with her toes, laughing when I'd jump. "Thank you for waiting for me."

"You are so worth the wait."

"So now what?"

We'd taken a leisurely shower and dressed after being so rudely–and terrifyingly? Embarrassingly?–interrupted by our progeny. I'm still not sure how I feel about the events of this morning, but Lena takes it all as if it were perfectly natural. It's one of her qualities I've always admired the most, her unshakeable confidence, her steady calm. It's hypnotic watching her go through life as though everything is just as it should be. Even when she had her cancer scare she'd faced it like, "Okay, what happens next?"; whereas, I was freaking out and doing my best not to show fear. I should know by now that she will always be strong enough for the both of us.

Apparently we'd taken just the right amount of time. Arabella and Beth had fixed all the breakfast treats and were still grumbling about having to cook when they'd come expecting to freeload.

"Andre's doing his laundry at home," Arabella says as we join them. "He said he'd be here in time to do the pancakes."

"Excellent," I say, popping a piece of bacon into my mouth. "Mmmm almost as good as mine."

"Hmph," Beth grunts. "Would have been better if it was waiting for me when I got here."

I grab her in a hug and squeeze her tight.

She squeezes me back tighter.

"Thanks, babe," I whisper in her ear.

"Are you happy, Mom?" She whispers back.

"Ridiculously."

We separate and she starts whisking the eggs.

The door opens and Andre waltzes in followed by the fourth and final member of the peanut gallery.

"Surprise!" Casey scoops me up and gives me a big hug, a shit-eating grin on his face. Since he was definitely my not-so-mini-me, I imagine he looks much like I looked a short time ago when his sister and best friends caught me in bed naked with *my* best friend.

"I didn't think you were coming," I say, but I'm thrilled.

"Georgia's spending the day with her mom, and once I got Andre's text, there was no way I was missing breakfast."

Ah. Conspiracy.

"Now that we're all here," Arabella says, hopping her butt up onto my counter. "We have some questions."

"You haven't made detective yet," Andre says, teasing his sister, our rookie police officer.

"It's okay," I say. "You're all entitled to some answers."

Lena chuckles as she pours herself some coffee. "Entitled is right."

Andre hip bumps her and she nearly spills her coffee.

"Guys! This is serious," Arabella says.

"Go ahead." I cross my arms over my chest, preparing for the onslaught. For a moment, my heart sinks and I wonder, what if they're really upset? What if they can't get behind this? What if Andre and Arabella don't want–

"Which one of you is moving?" Arabella finally asks.

"Yeah, and if it's Mom," Andre says, "Is she taking the TV? Cause if not–"

"All you care about is the TV? What about our childhood home?" Arabella asks. "What about–"

Lena and I crack up. We should have known our kids would react this way.

"Guys," Lena interrupts. "This..." She gestures between us as she takes her place next to me. I like it. I like being able to just slip my hand around her waist and hold her close to me. It's weird, but I like it. "This is only about ten hours old. Nobody's talking about selling houses yet."

"Yet," I echo. "I'm thinking we might want to keep that TV. It'll be great out on the deck with the hot tub."

"You're right! I can watch football and relax in style."

"We can put the extra fridge out there too, right next to the hot tub so we don't even have to get out for beer."

We high five and the kids stare at us like we've lost our minds.

I definitely like it.

Andre starts pouring pancake mix on the griddle while Lena does more brainstorming about how to combine our households. Casey votes for Lena's couch to sit on the deck so he can watch the game too. We pile all of the goodies on our plates and make our way to the dining room table, which has always been set up to seat eight. Our families have always been close, and will continue to be, no matter what Lena and I choose to do.

I sit at the head of the table and Lena sits to my right. She takes my hand in hers and I pull her over to kiss her, thrilled that this is my life. Everything else is details we can work out later. Or, there's always running away. She wiggles her eyebrows at me and I figure she'd agree to anything as long as we're together.

She's the most beautiful woman I've ever seen.

She's my best friend.

And I'm hopelessly in love with her.

Good thing she feels the same.

Cassidy's Return

Liz Faraim

My law firm had taken on a complex case, and I was knee-deep in litigation prep, so taking a quick trip to New York wasn't the best use of my time. Yet, the chance to reconnect with Marie over the Fourth of July holiday was an opportunity I couldn't pass up.

I managed to get plenty of work done on the long flight from Los Angeles and was pleased with the new business-class accommodations on the airline. My seat was fairly spacious and included a large writing surface and charging ports. What displeased me was the casualness of the clerk at the car rental station when she addressed me as *Honey* and *Ma'am* instead of Miss Watkins. To top it off, I had reserved a Mercedes SUV, and all they had for me was a Range Rover. Rather than make a fuss, I took what was available and made a note to leave them a poor review when I had time.

It had been a long day of travel, and I found myself battling some nerves about seeing Marie, who had been my lover in college.

My mood settled as I got clear of the city and passed into the greenery of the north shore of Long Island. Old stone churches, tunnels formed by the trees overhead, and meadows of wildflowers all served to bring me back to baseline.

With a faint smile, I turned into the driveway of the Sterling Shores Country Club. The massive wrought iron gates were open. I drove slowly through the arched stone gateway and was comforted to see the sprawling, immaculately manicured lawns. I hadn't been to the club in decades, but at first glance, nothing seemed to have changed. Even the hand-hewn granite paving stones edging the grass were the same.

I took my time driving down the lane past the tennis courts and pro shop at the top of the hill, whose buildings were painted a deep green to help them blend in with the tall trees and lush landscape. I grinned at the familiar sound of rackets hitting balls and tennis shoes sliding on clay courts.

Past the courts, the lane was lined with tall trees on the left and a golf course fairway on the right. Golfers, dressed all in white, discussed club selections with their caddies. In the distance was the country club itself, sandwiched between marshland and an expanse of water that was the Long Island Sound.

Small white signs, neatly hand-lettered in dark green paint, informed me that the speed limit was ten miles per hour, and I stuck to it despite the Range Rover wanting to zoom along. Halfway down the hill, I came across two children dressed in white tennis skirts and polos, with tennis rackets slung over their shoulders, thumbing a ride. I was thrilled to see that catching a ride was still something the kids at the club did. The innocence and relative safety of the insulated environment allowed that practice to live on.

I pulled to a stop beside them, and they hopped into my backseat without hesitation.

"Hello, ladies." I looked at them in my rearview mirror. "Coming back from tennis lessons?"

"Yes," they both chirped as I drove on.

The girls chattered away in the backseat, discussing Harry Styles' outfit choices at a recent concert. With a press of one button, I rolled all the windows down, letting in the fresh ocean air accented with hints of cut grass.

"Are you two excited for the fireworks tonight?" I asked.

"Oh yes, it's my favorite thing in the whole wide world," said the younger one.

The older girl elbowed her. "Last night you said chocolate ice cream was your favorite thing in the whole world."

"You two wouldn't happen to be sisters, would you?" I asked.

"Uh-huh," they both said, their tawny heads bobbing as they nodded.

I pulled to a stop in the gravel parking lot at the end of the road, surprised that the lot had not been paved after all those years. I was sure people had complained about the gravel damaging the paint jobs of their luxury SUVs and sports cars. Maybe the club left it unpaved to ensure people followed the speed limit.

"Have a great evening, you two," I said.

The girls hopped out. "Thanks for the ride."

I watched them jog away before I parked. The vehicle automatically folded in its side mirrors as I checked my hair and teeth in my compact.

I sighed, pushing away a twinge of anxiety as I set the car alarm. My light summer dress rippled in the breeze, and gravel crunched under my sandals as I walked across the lot to the porter seated at a podium.

Not recognizing me as a regular member, he sat up straight on his stool and gave me a thorough look from head to toe, no doubt checking to make sure I was following the dress code. Sitting under a massive shade umbrella, his starched shirt and khaki shorts were flawless despite the humidity and heat. His silver-plated name tag informed me that his name was Frederick.

"Good afternoon, Miss." He had an upper-crust drawl that I wasn't expecting.

"Good afternoon. I have been invited as a guest of Marie Miller." I placed a visitor pass on the glossy green top of his podium.

"Very good." He jotted down a note with a small golf pencil on a clipboard and tucked away my visitor pass. "Before entering, please read the visitor rules and sign at the bottom."

He produced an iPad and turned it to face me.

> *Club Dress Code*
> *Smart club attire is required. Dress should be appropriate to a country club atmosphere. Denim blue jeans are not permitted at any time. The staff will enforce this code. Hats should be worn with the brim facing forward and removed when entering indoor facilities. Gentlemen of all ages are required to wear collared shirts except in the pool area or on the beach.*
>
> *Cell Phone Policy*
> *Talking on cell phones, texting, emailing, and checking digital content on any device is strictly prohibited anywhere on Club property except in cars and in the designated "cell phone areas."*
>
> *Social Media Policy*
> *Please refrain from naming the club or its location on any form of social media. Please disable the location services on your phone or other devices when posting photos on social media.*

I picked up the stylus, my freshly manicured nails glinting, and signed my name on the screen.

> *Cassidy Watkins*

I pulled my cell phone out and powered it down.

Frederick nodded, satisfied. "Miss Watkins, welcome to Sterling Shores." He slid a paper map across the podium to me.

"That won't be necessary, Frederick. I spent many summers here as a child. Thank you."

He nodded and gave me a sun-wrinkled smile, motioning that I could pass. I stepped out from under the protection of his sun umbrella and strode halfway across a footbridge before pausing. I looked down at the shallow water of the creek below, the sun flashing off breeze blown ripples on its surface. When I was a child, my mother told me that each of those glints was an angel dancing with joy. The fond memory of my late mother brought a swell of happiness to me, despite my staunch atheism as an adult.

I walked on, a small thrill in the pit of my stomach as I passed the massive barrier hedges and went into the beach club area. To my right was the Olympic-sized pool that I had spent countless hours in for both recreation and competition. The pool was a hub of activity as children jumped from the diving boards and splashed about while parents and nannies watched from chairs on the pool deck. A deeply tanned lifeguard in red swim trunks sat under an umbrella, a smoldering cigar in one hand and an iced coffee in the other. Nothing had changed.

To my left were two horseshoe-shaped sections of cabanas, and straight ahead was the clubhouse, the sands of the beach peeking out along the side.

"Cassidy, welcome," Marie said as she waved to me from a table outside the clubhouse.

I immediately blushed as Marie strode toward me dressed in a flowing white blouse, bikini straps visible at the shoulders, and a glamorous sarong around her waist.

"Hello, Marie," I said, leaning into her hug, breathing the scent of her coconut sun oil. "Thanks for having me."

"Of course. How long has it been since you have been to the club?" she asked, lacing her arm through mine chummily as we walked.

"At least twenty years."

The familiar sounds of the halyard clanging against the metal flagpole and golf cleats clicking on the pavement brought back the comforts of a carefree childhood.

We passed the open-air snack bar, which smelled like French fries, and followed a short walkway to the beachfront cabanas. I raised my eyebrows subtly, knowing how exclusive the beachfront cabanas were. They were typically passed down generations and were very difficult to attain. My family had a cabana closer to the pool, which was a smidge lower down the pecking order.

The irony that there was a class structure, even at a place where everyone was exceptionally wealthy, wasn't lost on me now. As a child, I was oblivious to the differences and had been more than happy with our accommodations.

The entire club seemed much smaller walking through it as an adult. The pathways are narrower, and the buildings are less grand. We reached Marie's cabana, which was part of a neat row of them, each with covered open-air seating areas out front and a small enclosed changing area and shower in the back.

The other cabanas in the row hadn't been opened for the day, their wicker furniture naked, and the doors to their huts closed. The seating area in front of Marie's was tasteful, with modern outdoor furniture, including two loveseats that faced each other with a low glass-topped wicker coffee table in between. The loveseat cushions popped with bright white and blue fabric reminiscent of Santorini and Mykonos.

"Beachfront, eh? I seem to remember your family used to have a cabana near mine," I said. I wanted to ask outright how she had gotten the upgrade but knew it would be considered bad taste to do so.

"This cabana has been in Chip's family forever."

I recoiled slightly at the mention of Chip.

"Have a seat. Relax," she said. She stepped into her cabana and opened a beautiful wooden cabinet.

I sat on the firm blue cushion, admiring the spotless sandy beach and rolling waves of the water. Fine lines striped the sand, having been raked by staff.

"Would you like a drink?" she asked.

I turned and was surprised to see that the antique wooden cabinet housed a wine fridge.

"Well, aren't you creative," I said with a laugh. "I'm sure the club manager would have a fit if he knew you had an illicit fridge in there."

"What he doesn't know won't hurt him." She gave me a sly wink. "I have a lovely prosecco. Want to give it a go?" she asked.

"I shouldn't, but yes."

She poured prosecco into delicate teacups, and we clinked the brims together as she sat cozily next to me.

"See, no one is the wiser. These teacups are the perfect camouflage."

"This place hasn't gone 'dry,' has it?" I asked.

"Oh God, no. They just want us to drink in the clubhouse, which is full of cigar smoke and nasty old men. No thanks."

"Ew," I said, taking a sip of the prosecco. The delicate bubbles danced on my tongue. "To clarify, the 'ew' was for the old men, not the prosecco."

Marie looked subtly from side to side and placed her hand on my thigh. My heart leaped, and I nearly dropped the teacup.

"I can't tell you how happy I am that you were able to make the trip to spend the holiday with me," she whispered.

"My pleasure. While I love living in California, I have missed the east coast."

"Just the coast?" she asked, raising an eyebrow playfully and leaning in closer, then thought better of it.

"More than the coast."

Her hand tightened on my thigh, and my heart quickened. We sipped our prosecco as my words floated between us until the sound of leather sandals slapping on the walkway broke the bubble. Looking over my shoulder, I saw a woman well into her 70s approaching at a fast clip. She was dressed in khaki capris and a stylish flowing white button-up blouse. A broad-brimmed floppy hat cast shade over her face and shoulders. A young porter followed, carrying a massive wicker picnic basket that looked to weigh as much as he did.

"Just put it down on the table there, young man," she said as she stopped in front of a cabana two doors away.

"Hello, Francesca," Marie called out, her silver bracelets tinkling as she gave a delicate wave.

"Hi, Marie," she replied. "Who is your friend?"

We stood and walked to Francesca's cabana. "Francesca, you may remember Cassidy Watkins."

Francesca tapped her lips with a glossy, manicured fingernail as she considered my name. A massive diamond ring hung loosely on her withered finger, only held in place by her knobby knuckle. The porter stood by, hands behind his back, waiting for instructions. Francesca ignored his presence the way only someone who grew up with household staff could.

"Watkins, Watkins. Hm." She removed her sunglasses and looked me up and down. "Yes, yes. You're the General's daughter, is that right?"

"Nice to see you again, Mrs. Mankini," I said.

"Such a shame. Your father didn't deserve what happened to him. That sort of scandal is not something any of us needs."

I bristled but forced myself to maintain the pleasant, carefree smile that was already on my face. In the courtroom, I was a bulldog, but I knew that wouldn't serve me well at Sterling Shores or with Mrs. Mankini.

Thankfully, the porter cleared his throat in an effort to either be dismissed or given a new task.

"You there, set up the cushions and sweep the sand out of my cabana."

"Yes, Mrs. Mankini," he said, his deeply tanned face showing relief at having something to do other than standby indefinitely listening to us talk.

He opened the double doors to her cabana and pulled out a pile of cushions, which he dutifully placed on her outdoor furniture. The cushions were a God-awful floral design that only a stuffy, old-money septuagenarian could love.

Marie and Francesca prattled on about the weather, the club's new tennis instructor, and finally, Francesca's granddaughter being accepted to Princeton. I nodded along and smiled, not the least bit interested, and watched the porter sweep the sand from Francesca's cabana back out onto the beach. Finished, he stood by again, waiting to be dismissed. I felt for him but knew it wasn't my place to remind Francesca of his presence.

I immediately tuned back in when I heard Francesca ask, "So, Marie, any children on the horizon for you and Chip?"

"We will see," Marie said noncommittally. "So wonderful to see you, Francesca. Enjoy your day."

"You too, dear."

We returned to Marie's cabana and the loveseat. My prosecco had grown warm and no longer dazzled my senses.

"Shall I top you off?" Marie motioned to my teacup.

"No, thank you." I was annoyed that Francesca had ruined the moment, but I resolved not to let the interaction spoil my whole evening and slapped on a fresh smile. "Actually, yes. Please do."

Marie slyly poured us fresh drinks.

"I can't believe she had the nerve to mention the scandal with your father," Marie said as she sat back down.

Not wanting to discuss it, I took a sip. "So, what is the agenda for tonight?"

"Dinner in the clubhouse at seven, then we can walk to the top of the hill for the fireworks display."

Francesca's sandals clapped along the pavement as she headed back toward the clubhouse, porter in tow, leaving us to ourselves.

"I couldn't help but overhear Francesca mention Chip. I thought you had told me you two are separated?"

Marie flapped a hand as if shooing away a fly. "Essentially, we are. He stays at the penthouse and works in the city all week. Most weekends, he doesn't make the trip out to the country to see me anymore. I am sure he has a mistress, or two, at this point."

The lawyer portion of my brain was waving red flags at me. "Yes, but is there anything filed with the courts yet? Anything in writing to document a formal separation?"

She sipped her prosecco, brown eyes on me. "No."

I let out an exasperated sigh and downed the last of my drink in one gulp, placing the delicate teacup on the table.

"Then why am I here?" Keeping my voice calm was a monumental task.

"You are here to spend a lovely Fourth of July evening with me. We'll have a nice dinner, watch the fireworks, and..." She squeezed my thigh.

I gently brushed her hand away. "That's adultery, and I want no part of it," I said firmly and stood to leave.

"Cassidy. Cass. Please." Marie's voice took on a pleading tone that I didn't know was even possible for her. "I... I'm so lonely. We don't have to get physical. Please stay."

My heart swelled for her. I'd never known Marie to show even an ounce of vulnerability, so for her to open up to me like that was unexpected. I needed a minute to collect my thoughts, looking out toward the shoreline. Two kids played in the surf while a few others swam out to the floating dock and slide. I pushed away memories of my own childhood, flying down that slide and splashing into the ocean. I sat on the other loveseat across from Marie.

I chose my words carefully. "I am glad to visit with you today as long as we keep it hands-off," I said, my voice softening.

"Thanks, Cass." She dabbed at a stray tear before it could fall and smear her mascara.

I tried to think of safe topics for conversation and decided our college sporting days were benign enough. "Have you heard from any of the Vassar swim girls? It's been so long since I've been in touch with them."

"Yes, they are all either off conquering corporate America or raising kids. Well, more like their nannies and au pairs are raising them, but I digress." She took a deep breath, seeming to reset herself, and smiled. "Whitney is on a diplomatic assignment in South America somewhere, Janet is CEO of that new electric car company, Hayley goes by Harlow now, and Kierstan has three or four kids that she adores and stays home with while her husband is in London for work." She gazed into the bottom of her empty teacup. "And then there's me. No kids. No career. Abandoned by my husband."

I wanted to wrap her up in my arms and comfort her, but I refrained, clutching my hands tightly in my lap.

"Abandoned? Don't you prefer it when he gives you space?"

"You're right. I'm just being dramatic. He is a good man, a true gentleman, and deserves a wife who wants to be with him. And that's not me. I can't even stand the thought of kissing him, his mustache scraping my lip. Or feeling his chest hair." She shivered. "I really should have known all those years ago that I was–" she lowered her voice to a whisper, "gay."

"Well, you know now. So, that should help guide your choices in the future."

"Ugh, you sound like such an attorney. But really, how did I not know?" She crossed her legs tightly. "I mean, come on. All those times in college, we traveled with the swim team, sharing hotel rooms. Dear God, Cassidy. You rocked my world."

Heat rose in my neck and face as I flushed at the memories. A chuckle escaped my lips. "Those were some fun times," I said, turning to watch the kids rocket down the floating slide, splashing into the water. Their faint whoops of joy reached us at the top of the beach.

"Do you know what I miss from my summers here as a kid?" I asked, trying to steer the conversation back to steady ground.

"Uh, let's see. Was it combing the beach for spent firework casings the morning after the Fourth of July festivities?"

"Haha, no, though that was always a good time. What I miss are the Dusty Millers at the snack bar. Do they still serve them?"

Marie's eyes brightened. "Let's go see," she said, hopping out of her seat.

"Really?"

"Of course. My treat. They still don't take cash or cards. Just write my cabana number on the chit, and they will put it on the tab."

We walked side by side to the open-air snack bar, the path narrow enough that our shoulders and hands nearly grazed. As much as I wanted to touch her, to take her hand, I made sure I didn't.

At the snack bar, children covered in sand and dressed in swimsuits, their wet hair plastered to their skulls, sat at the tables eating French fries and grilled cheese sandwiches just like I used to do.

I stepped up to the counter, which was a thick slab of highly varnished wood, and nodded to the stoic teenager on the other side. He was clean-shaven, and his white polo shirt was buttoned to the top. His name tag said Gavin.

"Do you serve Dusty Millers?" I asked.

"Yes, Miss. We do," he said, all business.

"Wonderful." I jotted my order down on the chit with a short golf pencil. "Anything for you, Marie?"

"I'd love a little nosh. I'll have a bowl of warm mixed nuts and an Arnold Palmer, please."

I noted her request and slid the chit across the bar to Gavin. He nodded and whisked the chit off to the back. We lingered near the counter, watching the waves until Gavin broke my reverie.

"Miss?"

I turned, and he dutifully slid a red tray across the bar toward me.

"Thank you, Gavin," I said.

"My pleasure, Miss. Let me know if you need anything else."

I nodded and smiled, turning to Marie. "Can we take this back to your cabana, or do we have to eat it here?" I asked.

"We can take it back."

I carried the tray, Marie half a step behind me, back to her cabana. I made sure to sit across the table from her again.

Her Arnold Palmer was served over ice in a tall clear glass with a thick wedge of lemon on the rim. The warmed mixed nuts were in a silver bowl and looked to be cashews, roasted peanuts, and smoked blanched almonds. My Dusty Miller looked amazing, a single scoop of high-quality vanilla ice cream in a little glass dish with a splash of hot fudge and a healthy dose of malt powder on top.

I picked up the bowl and used a petite silver spoon to get a bit of ice cream, fudge, and malt powder. Sliding the delicate bite into my mouth, I stifled a groan. Each element was just as I remembered. Everything melted together in my mouth. I closed my eyes and couldn't stop myself from remembering so many days as a small child in a wet swimsuit, sitting at the snack bar eating a Dusty Miller, my only worry was not to get stung by jellyfish when I got back in the water.

"Oh my gosh. This is amazing." I took another delicate bite.

Marie nodded, eating nuts daintily and watching me. "You're eating dessert before dinner. That's so unlike you, Cassidy."

"What do you mean?"

"You've always been very black and white. Always followed the rules and did things in the proper order. No wonder you became a top-notch attorney."

"Well, today's a special occasion. Maybe I am trying to revive some of those good childhood memories a bit."

She took a sip of her Arnold Palmer and pointed at me. "I like it. I like seeing you dipping your toe into the gray area. Coloring outside of the lines."

I laughed. "Eating some ice cream before dinner is me coloring outside of the lines?"

"Live a little, Cass."

I savored the last bite of my Dusty Miller and nearly choked when the dinner gong rang, startling me.

"Come on, time to eat." Marie stood, stretching her arms over her head. The hem of her shirt rose, exposing the deeply tanned skin of her abdomen and hips.

I pushed down the desirous thoughts that surfaced, reminding myself that she was still married, thus off limits.

We walked at a leisurely pace to the clubhouse, allowing the families with children and older members to go in before us. There was no rush because the seating was assigned. I was relieved to see people with children seated away from us on the lanai, but I was slightly annoyed to see that we were seated at a large round table with Francesca and several moldy old men who were puffing on cigars. I grieved for my dress and wondered how long it would take my dry cleaner to get the stink of smoke out of the fine fabric.

Dinner was a blur of lobster bisque, apple cider brined pork chops with caramelized leeks, and a delightful green salad with grated apple. I opted to skip the wine, sticking with Pellegrino.

Francesca held court throughout the meal, regaling the men with stories of her last safari. At one point, she tried to get a conversation going with me and the old guys about my dad, but I tactfully dodged that. For the rest of the meal, I stayed quiet, happy to be ignored.

Marie and I excused ourselves before the dessert course, elbows occasionally rubbing as we walked out of the clubhouse and up the lane to the top of the hill. Several porters in golf carts offered us rides to the seating area, but we declined, preferring to walk. The evening cooled a few degrees, and the humidity settled as the sun set.

At the top of the hill, in the middle of the fairway, an area was sectioned off for people to sit. There were already a couple of families sitting on blankets, the nannies and au pairs trying to get the children to sit still long enough to eat a picnic dinner while the parents looked on, sipping from champagne flutes.

"Good evening, Mrs. Miller. Seating for two?" asked a porter.

"Yes, thanks," Marie said.

"Would you like deck chairs or a blanket?"

Marie looked at me, and I shrugged, indifferent.

"A blanket, please." Marie paused. "Can we be seated away from the family area?" she whispered.

The porter winked at her conspiratorially. "Very good," he said and spread a green and white checked blanket on the grass, away from the children.

"Thank you." Marie slipped him a twenty-dollar bill.

As we watched the sunset fade and turn to dusk, an army of golf carts arrived with the remaining people from the clubhouse. Thankfully, most of the golf cart riders chose to sit in deck chairs, which were set up behind us, so we still managed to have a bit of our own space.

Spread before us was the darkened shoreline of the Long Island Sound. A few errant fireworks popped up from neighboring beaches.

The lead porter tapped a silver spoon against a wine glass, and the small crowd quieted down. "Ladies and gentlemen, in honor of Independence Day, we present to you the Sterling Shores' annual fireworks display, which will begin momentarily. On behalf of the board of directors, please enjoy."

Other fireworks displays began dotting the shoreline to our left and right. A little girl in a corduroy jumper, oblivious to the explosions in the sky, walked dreamily past our blanket with her hands extended. After a moment of watching, I realized she was trying to catch a firefly. With great patience, she followed the insect as it flew drunkenly along until she closed her hands delicately around it. The bug lit up, and the little girl's hands glowed. She giggled excitedly.

"Nice catch," I whispered to her.

She looked at me, her eyes full of wonder, before running back to her family's blanket to show off her treasure, veering toward the nanny instead of her parents.

Marie chuckled.

"What?" I asked with a smile.

"Do you remember that one Fourth of July when your dad carved a huge castle out of Styrofoam? Our folks floated it out into the Sound and shot it with flaming tennis balls full of gasoline."

I groaned. "How could I forget! God, I can't imagine anyone thinking that would be a good idea now. I don't even want to think about how much pollution that burning Styrofoam did to the air and water. Our parents must have been absolutely out of their minds. But hey, it did look pretty flaming on the water under the night sky, with fireworks up and down the coast all around us."

"That was the first time you kissed me. Do you remember?"

I did remember, and a bolt of electricity shot from my chest to the palms of my hands at the thought of it.

"We were just silly kids," I said, pushing away the urge to get romantic with her.

The smile faded from Marie's face, and I knew I had hurt her. My brain scrambled for something to say that would make it all better, but before I could speak, the sky overhead erupted as the fireworks began. The smaller children shrieked in surprise while the adult guests let out a collective, "Oooh."

Marie leaned back on her elbows and tugged my arm, so I leaned back as well. The Sterling Shores show was spectacular, as always. They spared no expense to put on an incredible performance for the small gathering.

I leaned toward Marie. "My favorite are the kind that make the crackling sounds and the one that looks like a weeping willow. How about you?" I asked, speaking into her ear so she could hear me over the explosions. Her hair still smelled of rosemary and tanning oil, and I wanted so badly to brush her hair away from her ear and kiss her neck, but I refrained.

She startled, breaking away from the trance of the fireworks, and turned to me so that we were nose to nose and smiled. She didn't speak, instead taking my hand and placing it over her racing heart.

A breeze blew in from the water, raising goosebumps on my skin. I wrapped us up in the blanket, slyly placing my hand back over Marie's heart. I knew that was as far as I would take it that night, but I longed for more.

As the pyrotechnics continued to awe the crowd, my mind drifted to the future. I would fly back to California first thing in the morning but knew that I would invite Marie to visit me in California as soon as she and Chip filed for separation. Thinking any further than that gave me a twinge of anxiety.

My independent lifestyle has done a good job of keeping my heart safe, but a certain pang rose in my chest at the thought of not giving it a go with Marie when the time was right. Seeming to sense my inner debate, Marie placed her hand over mine, pressing it between the warm skin of her chest and her palm, and my mind was made up.

Garden Party

Richard May

"Henry, what you doin' for Labor Day?" my friend and colleague Bill Barnes drawled at me after plopping his long, lean body onto one of the green fabric chairs facing my desk.

"Nuthin," I drawled back at him, which wasn't precisely true. I had an invitation to drive home to Nashville for a family picnic, but that could wait if Bill Barnes had a better idea.

"Good," he said, slapping his well-tailored thighs and standing up. "You are coming home with me then. We can leave work early on Friday. Old Man Lafferty's bound to announce an early closing. Bring a suit or two. We still on for lunch?"

I nodded, sitting back in my chair. A weekend with Bill Barnes, in his home territory. Well, I swan–as my granny used to say. The possibilities made it difficult for me to concentrate on the Smallsby case at hand. I had wanted Bill Barnes since I'd joined Lafferty, Williams, and Wattley three years before and I had heard about his family's house, with its fluted columns and full-frontal verandah, often enough to wonder whether it truly existed. The wanting and the house had come together in my mind.

On the day, bags in hand, we ambled through the heat and humidity toward the parking garage, Bill Barnes talking all the way. Mr. Lafferty had indeed let the staff leave early and given us attorneys the option. Normally, I might not have taken it, but I would follow Bill Barnes anywhere, anytime.

I gave God a little thank-you Bill had a convertible. The weather was so hot and heavy I had already sweat through my dress shirt. We tossed our bags in the Audi's trunk and headed south on US 61–the Blues Highway, Bill said–with the top down, through fields of farmers' market gardens. I'd been to some on weekends. That was about as far south in Mississippi as I had been until now.

"Do you like the blues?" I asked.

"Not really. How about you?"

"Some," I answered, staring at the mound of his left pectoral exposed by the wind sluicing through the car, made possible by Bill undoing at least three buttons after he removed his tie. "I'm looking forward to meeting your family," I said, trying to take my mind off Bill Barnes's chest.

He gave me a funny look, but it vanished, and he slapped my thigh. "Hope you like crowds!" he exclaimed.

Just north of Clarksdale, a town I'd only seen previously on a map, we did a jog west and then south again on a narrow state highway flanked by telephone poles along one side and a line of cottonwoods on the other. We drove fast through one disintegrating little Southern town after another until Bill announced, "Here we are! Rosedale, Mississippi, my hometown." I had imagined antebellum mansions and rolling lawns, given Bill's often recited family history, so Rosedale with its rundown, ruined, and empty storefronts was disappointing. I wasn't sorry when Bill didn't stop.

On the other side of town, we passed through a brief thicket of sweet gums and more cottonwoods into a wide field of low green plants. "What's that?" I asked, nodding right.

"Our soybeans," Bill answered. "We're close to Beaulieu now."

He eased the car around a curve, and the air grew heavier still. I could see the Mississippi on our left, through groves of cypress trees. At a promising drive, we turned right, passing under monstrous oak trees hung with Spanish moss into a clearing with a grand two-story exceptionally white mansion at its center. Beaulieu did not disappoint. It had the requisite four columns and a second-story verandah. Two wide wings flanked the center, like bodyguards. We had landed in antebellum country at last.

"Is this Beaulieu?" I asked, just to make sure.

"Nah, son, we're just stopping to ask directions," Bill deadpanned before he whacked my shoulder and grinned at me. He eased the Audi into a parking space between a Lexus and a Buick and honked three times. People ran from the house, yard, and who knows where to greet us, all talking at once.

"Billy! You're late!" yelled a young woman who could have been his twin, all sunny hair and laughing face. I made a note of her nickname for Bill Barnes; I might be able to use it one day. Others shouted similar greetings, except one darker young man. He hung back, as if he were shy or not really part of the group.

"Y'all, this is my friend, Henry Williams from Nashville," Bill said to the assembled dozen or more. They all yelled "Hello!" or "Welcome!"–even the dark-haired man. I saw his lips move, and pretty lips they were.

"Henry, let me introduce you to my cousin Jamie," Bill Barnes said, wading through the crowd toward the solitary figure. "Jamie Battle, this is Henry Williams. You'll like him." The two of us shook hands, both wondering, I suppose, what that meant. But then I was swept away to meet more cousins, two sisters, a brother-in-law, Bill's mother and father, and an uncle and aunt. No one else looked like Jamie Battle, even the brother-in-law. They were all golden, like Bill Barnes. Maybe Jamie Battle was adopted. His olive skin and dark curly brown hair stood out among the fair-complected Barneses.

We flowed up the broad steps, across the spacious front porch and into the house, where I found myself in an eddy alongside Jamie Battle. "I'll show you to your room," he said softly. It surprised me he would be my guide, but Bill was busy with his family, so I followed the cousin up the wide, dark oak staircase which bisected the first floor to the second-floor landing.

"Billy thought you'd like this room," Jamie Battle said as we turned down a right-angled hall into the east wing. "It's a little more private and a little quieter," he added, as if he could tell how overwhelmed I was by the Barnes family at full volume.

"Thank you," I said. I modulated my voice to match his softer tones.

The room Jamie Battle opened the door to was large and high-ceilinged. I wondered if all the bedrooms were like this at Beaulieu. Maybe I'd see at least one other of them while I was visiting if my hopes for the weekend with Billy Barnes were realized.

"Lovely," I said.

"Thank you," Jamie Battle responded, as if the compliment were for him.

I walked to the three tall open windows. Below was a beautiful rose garden in soothing pastels.

I said the obvious, "What beautiful roses!"

Jamie stepped next to me and turned his hazel eyes my way. The color brought up memories: my first boyfriend had hazel eyes. I had a peculiar urge to tell Jamie Battle that but decided it was best not to go there.

"Thank you," he repeated. "My grandmother tends it, although she does ask me to do the heavy work. I like the colors." He leaned closer to the screen just as a breeze rushed through the room, ruffling his shirt. It was open three buttons, just like Bill Barnes' on the trip down. In a glimpse, I saw a well-developed chest, black curly hair covering it, and one tight, small brown nipple. I looked up into Jamie Battle's eyes. He gave me a sweet smile. I made some quick, nervous conversation.

"You live here then. Did I meet your grandmother?" Jamie Battle's smile became guarded.

"Yes," he confirmed. "I live here." He turned back to the garden below us. "Nana's probably resting from the heat. But she'll be down to supper, I expect." The rhythm of his voice changed, a cadence I couldn't quite place. We stood next to each other for a minute, staring at the roses.

"Well, then," he finally said, with a sigh as regretful as I felt. "I'll leave you in peace. Supper is at eight, dinner at noon, and breakfast any ol' time. Fridays we always dress, and we have the garden party Monday of course. Oh, did Billy…?"

"Yes," I answered, interrupting. "I brought a suit." In truth, I had brought several.

He looked me up and down, taking his time. "I was going to offer you one of mine. We're about the same size." I felt something stirring but wasn't exactly sure whether it was in my host or me. Before we could explore that one way or the other, Jamie Battle excused himself and left the room. I was left alone with regret and the beginning of an inkling why.

I heard Bill Barnes' loud voice accost Jamie Battle in the hallway, with his soft murmurs answering. In another two seconds, Bill was striding into my room. He closed the door behind him, with a wink. I became suddenly conscious that we were alone, at least for the moment, and there was a bed in the room. "The rose bedroom!" he proclaimed. "I told Jamie Battle you'd like it." He joined me at the window, leaning against the frames, ignoring the garden, no breeze entering now. "How do you like him?" he asked.

"Your cousin?" Bill nodded. "He's nice. Very striking. He doesn't look much like the rest of y'all." I hurried to explain myself. "I mean, you're all so blond and he's…"

"Not," Bill finished for me, looking as if he'd could go on but not clear he should. "There's a story there," he said after a few moments of uncharacteristically biting his tongue. "But I best let Jamie Battle tell it. Would you like a shower before you dress?" My heart leaped, hoping that was some kind of sexual invitation, but Bill made no move to disrobe. I unbuttoned my shirt, watching him watch me. *Maybe now,* I said to myself, but Bill just sort of snapped to attention, said he'd see me in a little while, and left. I continued taking my clothes off, feeling regretful for the second time in fifteen minutes.

Cocktails were served at six p.m. on the back lawn. We were surrounded by massive willows swaying gently side-to-side like hoopskirts in the occasional breeze. I noticed an older woman, bent slightly with age, standing on her own in a far corner. She was very pale but with African hair and features. I couldn't imagine who she might be until Jamie Battle joined her and took her arm. I saw then immediately.

They walked slowly toward me, at the old woman's pace. "Mr. Henry Williams," Jamie Battle began once they'd reached me. "I'd like to introduce you to my grandmother, Mrs. Annabelle Watts." She smiled and extended a slender hand, brown with liver spots.

"Pleased to meet you, Mr. Williams," she said in a soft soothing voice not unlike her grandson's in tone. Her eyes were a warm brown, and the smile creases around them and her lips told me she had led a happy life, or at least that she was optimistic.

"As am I to meet you, Mrs. Watts," I said, bowing over her hand, feeling like quite the Southern gentleman. She withdrew hers from mine gracefully and asked about my family, which, black or white, is what Southerners do.

I explained I was from Nashville, that my parents were both living, and I had two sisters and a brother, all married and spread from Austin to Atlanta.

"It's hard, isn't it, not to be with family," she said, telling me, if I didn't know already, that she was not a Barnes. "I do miss my own people."

"Where are they, Mrs. Watts?" I asked politely.

"Do you know Arcola?" she asked. I said I didn't. "It's down in Washington County. Not far really." Her voice trailed off. "But Beaulieu is so pretty I couldn't say no when my grandson invited me to live with him. I have my own house." She examined my reaction. I struggled with the sudden understanding: Jamie Battle owned Beaulieu.

We were interrupted by a servant with the sheen of purple, who appeared at Jamie Battle's side and said something into his ear. Jamie turned from us to his relatives gathered on the lawn beyond. "Supper's ready, everyone!" he called in a loud, strong voice. That confirmed he was the master of the house.

Supper was in a wide room beautifully wallpapered in a green pattern, with illumination sconces along the walls and a long, well-preserved oak table down its center. Jamie Battle had me sit next to his grandmother, who was on his left. Bill Barnes was on his right, a disruption of the otherwise male, female, male, female seating arrangement. That made me wonder if the two men were more than relatives. Maybe that's why Bill Barnes flirted with me but didn't follow through.

During a fine meal of beef bourguignon, hearty red wine, and ambrosia that reminded me of my mother's, I chatted comfortably with Mrs. Watts and, at a much higher volume, with my neighbor on the left, one of the several cousins. Bill Barnes and Jamie Battle kept up a steady conversation in whispers, extending my suspicions.

After supper, our host excused himself as he stood up. "I'll just escort Nana home," he explained.

Mrs. Watts took my hand. "A pleasure to meet you, Mr. Williams. How long are you staying, did you say?"

"Just the weekend," I replied, feeling sad to admit it.

She smiled. "Perhaps you'll come visit me before you go. Come for dinner tomorrow. The two of you," she said, glancing with meaning toward her grandson. I looked at him as well but with questions.

"We will," he promised her, without returning my look.

Mrs. Watts smiled Jamie's smile at me before she took his arm and they slowly departed the dining room, calling good night to everyone and being wished good night in return.

"Now you know," Bill Barnes's jaunty voice said at my elbow. "Come have a whiskey with me." His hand latched onto my arm and pulled me away with him into the flow of Barneses leaving the dining room.

In the family parlor, he and I saluted each other and took a sip from heavily etched glasses. "He is my cousin," Bill said, as if I'd told him I didn't believe it. "Uncle Stephen's boy." I waited while he chugged his drink, as if he had to do that before he could go on. "His mother was Black," he confided after he swallowed. Not Aunt Whoever, just "his mother." And Black, as if that summed her up. I was tempted to comment but decided it was Barnes business, not mine. I suppose I was meant to be shocked.

"Where do they live?" I asked, stifling things I might have said I might have regretted. I still had salacious hopes for the weekend.

"They died," Bill Barnes said bluntly. He poured more Jack Daniels into my glass and refilled his with Maker's Mark. "Stephen was the oldest son so Jamie inherited," he said. "Lucky for us he didn't want to sell." He leaned his head back and emptied half of the new glassful.

"He lives here alone?" I asked.

"Yes, suh," Bill said, with an already imprecise enunciation. "Jamie Battle Barnes lives in this big ol' house all alone." He swept his free arm around the room to illustrate his statement, wobbling a bit on his feet. He downed another big slug of whiskey, staring at me over the glass. I felt I was supposed to ask a question or maybe make a suggestion. If I hadn't seen what I had at supper, I might have. Bill Barnes looked mighty fetching in his summer gray.

"He's not married?" I asked instead.

Bill almost snorted his drink out his nostrils. "Let's just say Jamie Battle is not the marrying kind, Henry," he answered, alternately coughing and chuckling. "Well, maybe now," he added, winking at me before he finished his drink. I wondered what that might mean, but we were joined just then by Bill Barnes's unmarried sister and their mother. I assumed this would be the beginning of the usual interrogatory—seeing if I were qualified as a prospective husband, but they just chatted amiably with Bill Barnes and me before leaving for other conversations. Bill poured himself another large drink.

When Jamie Battle entered the room, Barneses ebbed and flowed around him, saying how well his grandmother looked. He thanked everyone politely while working his way across the room to us. Bill Barnes poured him a double shot of Maker's.

"Your grandma is looking hale and hearty, cousin," Bill offered, along with the drink. "Her arthritis not acting up?"

"Some," Jamie said. "But not as bad as last spring. Thank you for asking." He turned to me. "Billy says you enjoy a swim." I agreed I did. "Maybe we can all go down to the river tomorrow morning while it's still cool," Jamie suggested. "Did you bring your trunks, Billy?"

"Yes, sir, and I made sure Henry Williams brought his, too. He looks quite nice in them," Bill Barnes answered, winking at me. My face turned beet red. "Aw, now, son. No need to be embarrassed. All those hours at the gym aren't just for your health, are they?"

The next morning, after breakfast, Bill Barnes followed me upstairs into my room and closed the door behind us again. My heart jumped hopefully for a second time. "How do you like Jamie Battle?" he asked again, after sprawling across my bed, already tidied up by unseen hands.

"I told you I like him fine," I replied, remaining standing, although I was sorely tempted to throw myself on top of him. I was tired of all show and no go. I guess my pique showed.

"What's wrong, son?" Bill asked, sitting up. I looked him in the eye. "Oh, Henry! You thought I asked you down here for myself? You know I'm not gay."

I decided to be stubborn. "Bill Barnes, you don't have a girlfriend. Haven't had one the whole time I've known you. Maybe you already have someone."

Bill returned my glare. "Henry Williams, if I were gay, you'd have known by now. And I don't already have someone. You'll be the best man when I do." He sounded serious. "Anyway." He rose quickly from the bed. "Get your swimsuit on. You brought the red one? Y'all looked so sexy at Mary McClain's pool party." I confirmed I brought the red speedo, per his instructions, and moved to get out of my clothes.

Bill didn't leave until I was down to my underwear. "No, sir, I would not have let all that get away," he said, wolf-whistling before he left the room.

A small group of us walked down the dusty drive and crossed the barely paved country road into the cypress trees along the river. Past the trees, there was a narrow beach and a short boat dock without a boat. We set our things on a convenient picnic table and all began to shed our clothes. I watched wistfully as Bill Barnes's sculpted body emerged from his T-shirt and shorts. He was wearing a speedo in a shade of blue that matched his eyes perfectly, if you looked closely, which I had. We were a noticeable contrast in our tiny swimsuits. Some of the women sported bikinis, but all the other men wore trunks.

Jamie Battle took the longest stripping down, and everyone seemed to watch. The mounds of his body curved more naturally than his cousin's, and his thighs were leaner than Bill's tree trunks but still nicely muscled. His forearms, face, and neck were darker than the rest of him, meaning he might be more than just a gentleman farmer. I pictured Jamie Battle plowing fields in a torn white T-shirt and dirty jeans, sweating in the sun. It was a fetching image. Behind me, I heard Bill Barnes chuckle and turned to see him watching me. He laughed out loud at my expression and ran for the river. The rest of us followed, and water sports began.

Afterward, lying on our towels, Jamie Battle on my left, I stole looks at our host's body and the arc of his lime-green trunks. "He's beautiful, isn't he?" Bill Barnes whispered into my ear from my right side, like the serpent to Eve. I was afraid to answer but whether because Jamie Battle would hear or the cousins, I wasn't sure.

"His mama and daddy were too. He looks some like both of them," Bill said, his hot breath making me hotter. It may have been my imagination, but I thought I felt Bill's tongue touch my ear.

"Really?" I said, surprised into turning my face so close to his we could have kissed. "I don't see much Barnes in him at all."

"Look closer," Bill advised, showing me a tip of the tongue I thought I'd felt. "It's there all right." I stared at Bill's mouth, fighting an urge to push my tongue into it, but I avoided making a fool of myself with Bill and looked at Jamie Battle. He smiled at me, as if he'd been listening, and I smiled back reflexively. I still didn't see any Barnes in him. I turned again to Bill, but he was on his back now, eyes and mouth closed, but since his body was open for inspection, I indulged myself from head to toe until Bill cleared his throat, interrupting my fantasies. I looked up from his prominent crotch to his face. One eye was open. It gave me a wink.

After we were dry, no one bothered putting their clothes back on for the short trip back to Beaulieu. The day was too hot already to care what we looked like. I walked with Bill, until he pushed me forward into Jamie Battle, making me land against his nearly naked body with a smack. "I'm sorry," I said, thinking how solid he was and how cool his skin felt, compared to the air around us.

"No problem, Henry," he said, smiling over his shoulder at me. I peeled myself off him and moved to his side. We fell into step.

He brought up dinner at his grandmother's. "Will you be ready by 11:30? My grandmother always eats at noon, when the whistle blows." He laughed, like he'd made a joke. "There isn't really a whistle. Not here at least. But in Arcola one always blew exactly at noon. Left over from slavery days," he said, his voice suddenly grim.

"I'll be ready," I promised, thinking about slavery myself. Had Jamie Battle's people been slaves at some point? Most likely. My own people had been dirt farmers during slavery, never rich enough to own other people, something I was thankful for.

At 11:28, my hand was on the doorknob when someone knocked on my door. I opened it and Jamie Battle and I were suddenly face-to-face, his lips almost as close to mine as Bill's had been at the river. I noticed they were as bee-stung as Bill's and most of his family. There was something Barnes about Jamie Battle after all.

"That's a lovely suit, Henry," he drawled softly, coolly looking down my body, as if in my room we were in a different world, his world. I felt the control in him, the deciding and waited. "Shall we go?" he asked after a few moments of looking from me to the windows to the bed and back at me. I nodded, a little dizzy from the tight hold of his attention.

Mrs. Watts' house was red brick, modest in comparison to Beaulieu but perfectly fine, all on one floor, with a full front porch, a parlor for receiving, a dining room, kitchen, and a fourth room behind a closed door, which I assumed shielded her bedroom.

"My grandson had this place built especially for me," she said proudly, after we were seated in the parlor. "My little house in Arcola wasn't anything as nice." She sounded wistful as she said it.

I looked at a covey of family photos on the upright piano, the faces becoming paler as the clothes became more modern. I particularly noticed one of a youngish couple, the woman dark-haired and olive-skinned, the man Barnes blond and more handsome than any of them. Mrs. Watts followed my eye.

"That was my daughter Beatrice and her husband, James Battle Barnes," she said, making an effort to get up. Her grandson hurriedly brought the photo to her, and she silently traced the features of her daughter with a loving forefinger.

"She was beautiful," I said when, with a sad smile, she handed the portrait to me.

"Jamie looks so much like his mother," Mrs. Watts said. "Although he has his father's kindness." I was surprised to hear *kindness* used about a Barnes. They were all perfectly nice, but *kind* was not a descriptive I would have chosen for any of them–except, perhaps, Jamie. I looked at the photo of James Battle Barnes a second time. His son looked more like him than at first glance, in the shape of the head maybe, and certainly in the eyes.

We helped Mrs. Watts serve coleslaw, black-eyed peas, cheese fritters, and ham. "Would you care for more iced tea?" she asked. I said I would, although it was a little sweeter than I preferred.

"Leave room for cobbler," Jamie advised with a loving look at his grandmother, as I took a second helping of black-eyed peas. The cobbler was peach, like my mother's best. I said yes to a scoop of vanilla ice cream on top. It was a holiday, after all. I'd be back in the gym Tuesday to begin countering all these calories.

"Thank you again, Mrs. Watts, for inviting me," I said, as Jamie and I were leaving. "Everything was delicious."

"You are most welcome, Mr. Williams," she said, with her hand in mine. Our handshake had turned companionable, although I hadn't been able to convince her to call me Henry. "I hope we'll have you back with us again real soon." She and Jamie Battle exchanged some silent communication in a quick look before we left.

Afterward, Jamie and I walked back toward Beaulieu, close enough that our elbows jostled. "Nana likes you," he said, hands in his trouser pockets. "She doesn't like everyone I introduce her to." I wondered if that meant other gay men or people in general.

"Do you ever get to Memphis?" I asked him after a silence full of unspoken sentences.

He gulped like I'd caught him in a lie. "Sometimes."

"Well, next time I hope you'll be my guest for supper. I don't live too far from Bill's. We could meet there. The three of us could go," I added, amused at my reluctance to include Bill now.

"Oh, I don't stay with Billy," Jamie said, brushing ever-present flies out of his face and not elaborating.

We walked almost to Beaulieu's front porch before Jamie Battle spoke again. "I'd love to see you in Memphis, Henry," he said to the air around us.

We climbed together up the wide front steps. He stopped me just below the porch with the barest touch of his fingertips on my sport coat and asked, "Will you sit by me at supper? I mean, if you need to sit with Billy, I understand." His brow was wrinkling with seriousness.

"Bill is just my friend," I told him. I didn't tell him I'd wished for years he'd be more than that. "I'd be very pleased to sit by you, Jamie." He smiled his thank-you, squared his shoulders, and walked up the remaining step into his home like there was something there he had to face.

That night, except for Mrs. Watts, we all went to Cleveland, about twenty miles east of Rosedale. It was a larger and much more attractive town, and the restaurant Jamie had chosen served surprisingly good Italian food. I rode with Bill Barnes in the convertible–Jamie Battle's SUV quickly filled without me–but at the restaurant I sat by Jamie Battle, as promised.

"My mother was a quarter Italian," Jamie said after he and I had ordered, as if I'd asked a question. I could see the Italian in him more than I could the Barnes. "My great-grandfather was in Italy during World War Two and brought back a war bride," he explained. "Where are your people from?" I'd heard this question often at school and in my professional life among the upper middle class not to think he meant location.

"Not too interesting, I'm afraid," I replied. "Scotch-Irish, Welsh, and English. Maybe a little Chickasaw."

"That's interesting about the Chickasaw," Jamie Battle said, looking at my light brown hair and letting his knee accidentally hit mine before he apologized and moved it away.

"It was a long time ago," I said. "Too many greats to remember. And it's probably just a family story anyway." I forced a laugh, which Jamie didn't join me in. After a moment, I asked why his grandmother wasn't at dinner with us.

"I was afraid she'd get too tuckered out," he answered. "Today was already mighty tiring for her, and I'm taking her to church tomorrow." He thought a moment. "Would you like to join us?"

I agreed to, wondering how Pentecostal the service would be. I was Methodist myself, at least when I went home to Nashville.

Bill had promised me a round trip in the Audi, but one of the aunts intervened, insisting on taking "a ride in that thing." Jamie Battle stepped in quickly to ask me to ride back with him and I accepted. Bill's younger sister volunteered to give me her seat up front with her cousin. She and miscellaneous family members filled the back two rows, laughing and talking raucously with one another.

Jamie drove fast through the dark over the narrow country byways, making me check my seatbelt, and we arrived at Beaulieu well ahead of the convertible. His family trooped into Beaulieu, calling to us to "hurry now." When I made to follow them, Jamie held my arm. His eyes were shining in the porchlight some servant must have turned on. "Would you like to take a walk?" he asked. I replied that a walk would be just the thing after a heavy dinner.

He led me across the road, through the cypress, back to the little beach and onto the dock. For a little while, we just stared down at the dark water drifting by but then Jamie gave me the same deciding look he'd had in my bedroom, took his shoes and socks off, and sat down on the edge of the dock. I sat next to him. Our bare feet dangled in the slow flow of the Mississippi. Waves rippled in the light of a nearly full moon. Our toes accidentally touched. Then, he was leaning, his head aiming for mine. The moonlight showed me his eyes were closed. Mine were wide open. His arms went around my back, and his hands explored its contours.

After the kiss and embrace, Jamie pulled away from me and exhaled. "I have wanted to do that ever since I first saw you," he said, with a gentle smile I was becoming accustomed to. I didn't know what to say or do. It didn't matter. We heard Bill Barnes' voice call from the little beach behind us.

"Henry? Jamie Battle? That you?" A flashlight shone in our faces and meandered down our bodies. Jamie Battle shielded his eyes with one hand.

"Shut that damn thing off, Billy," he said, sounding irritated for the first time since I'd met him. The flashlight quickly went dark.

"Sorry, boys. Thought y'all mighta got lost. Coming in or y'all gonna stay out here all night?" he asked slyly.

It was a suggestion I realized in an instant I could happily take, but Jamie Battle muttered, "I suppose we better go in, Henry," so I dried my feet with my socks and put them and my shoes back on. Jamie Battle stuffed his socks in his shoes and carried them across the road to Beaulieu. Bill Barnes led the way with the flashlight.

Inside the house, music was playing in the family parlor–light jazz, a little bluesy. Bill Barnes poured three glasses. "Maker's for you, Jamie," he said, handing him one. "And Jack for the gentleman from Tennessee." He clinked mine after I'd taken it. I stopped short of saying I wasn't a gentleman. I know some fictions have to be maintained.

"To you," Bill said, toasting us together, with a leering grin. The three of us tipped our glasses back in unison, all seeming to need a drink. By the time parents, sisters, one sister's husband, uncle, aunts, and cousins had gone up to bed, Jamie Battle, Bill Barnes, and I had knocked back several more.

"Guess I'll go up too," I said after the last cousin had left. I hoped Jamie Battle heard the regret in my voice.

"Nah. The night is young, boys," Bill said, slurring his words. We had one more with him before he fell asleep. Then, Jamie and I hauled him upstairs, his arms over our shoulders, and deposited him on his double bed with a whomp.

"Should we take his clothes off?" I whispered to Jamie Battle, thinking of all the times I'd wanted to.

"I reckon so," he answered. He worked on Bill's shirt while I removed his shoes and socks. I let Jamie unzip his pants, but I pulled them down Bill's thick legs, feeling the muscles as I went. He was a sight, sprawled on the bed in only his briefs. I wanted to lie down next to him, but Jamie Battle and I left him snoring.

In the hall outside his cousin's room, Jamie and I hesitated. After several awkward moments, he gave me a quick kiss, a quicker squeeze, and said, "Good night." I watched him walk off in the opposite direction from mine.

In my room, I undressed slowly in the dark and lay on top of my bed, considering the day and listening to frogs plead for rain. A low breeze swept over me through the open windows like Jamie Battle's fingers on the dock. I thought of him while I drifted off to sleep but, with a start, I woke back up. My door was opening. A dark figure stepped into the room, shutting the door quietly behind it. I watched it walk toward the bed. "Jamie?" I asked expectantly.

"Nah, son. It's Bill Barnes." He settled onto the bed beside me. "Thought I'd try this gay thing out," he said, reaching for my body.

"Bill…" I started to say, before his mouth covered mine and reduced my words to a mumble. He deftly removed my underwear and hid it under a pillow.

"You surely do feel good, Henry," Bill Barnes said, shifting his body on top of mine. He was naked. "Did y'all bring condoms?" I thought of all the nights I had wanted this and didn't fight when he pushed my legs apart with his thighs.

Just then, my door opened a second time and another figure entered the room. "Henry, you awake?" It was Jamie Battle.

"Come on over, cousin," Bill said. "Let's have us a threesome. Never did that with two guys before."

The second figure rushed back out of the door immediately. I pushed Bill Barnes off me and ran after Jamie, naked as the day I was born. I caught him by the arm just as he was going into his room. "Jamie!" I said too loudly. He scowled and put a finger to his lips. "That wasn't my idea," I told him, whispering emphatically. "Bill, I mean. He came in just before you did. Honest." I didn't tell him that, if he had arrived two minutes later, he would have seen Bill Barnes and I connected in an undeniably mutual way.

Jamie didn't answer, but he didn't pull away either. After a long look between us, he ushered me into his room with one hand behind my back and shut the door after us with the other one. The next moment his hands were all over me, grabbing my chest, gripping my back, sliding down my legs and holding on. They felt a little rough, calloused by work, but good, like the boys of summer at my grandparents' farm. He kissed down my neck and across my chest, lips counting my abs. When he took me whole into his mouth, I gasped. "Jamie!" I said, leaving a verbal ellipsis.

When he deemed me ready, he stood up, undid his robe, and let it drop onto the floor behind him. "Have you ever been with a Black man, Henry?" he asked, his voice solemn in the dark, his arms across his chest.

"You're hardly Black," I answered.

"But I am, Henry. By the drop of blood rule for one thing but more than that..." he started to say. I put a hand to his lips.

"I have been with Black men," I lied, to avoid a discussion. That seemed to be the right answer. We went hand in hand to his bed and lay down side by side. Jamie's hands traced the contours of my body, as if he were mapping them for future reference. I touched his cheek and felt down his body, taking him in hand. He made low sounds which might have been words. Without words or sounds, he turned me onto my other side and slid behind me. I was ready.

He pulled away.

"What's wrong?" I asked over my shoulder.

"I don't want to hurt you," he told me. "I'm big." I wondered if that were the Barnes in him Bill had alluded to. I had recent evidence from Bill mounting me.

"Go ahead," I told him.

The next morning, I woke to Jamie Battle smiling at me. His arms were still around me, but we were face to face. "Now you've been with a Black man," he said when he saw I was awake, as if he knew I'd been lying.

"I surely have," I replied, not trying to be coy. He looked over my shoulder at the time.

"We better get ready for church," he said. "Do you want to shower first?"

"Why don't we shower together?" I suggested. I borrowed a robe, and we managed to avoid any scandal to and from.

Surprisingly, most of the other Barneses joined us for Sunday services, except Bill, who as yet hadn't been seen. I rode with Jamie Battle and his grandmother to the simple, high-steepled building Bill Barnes and I had passed in Rosedale on our way to Beaulieu. Grace Episcopal, the sign said. There wouldn't be any hand-raising or speaking in tongues after all. I swore at myself for thinking in stereotypes.

During the service, I could not stop appreciating how handsome Jamie Battle was in his light-blue linen suit, crisp white shirt, and multi-colored tie. His black hair, so rumpled and astray during our night, was sleekly combed and gleaming with gel. From time to time, Mrs. Watts peeked around him at me. Each time, she smiled and settled back out of view with happy eyes.

After services, we had breakfast in a café crowded with dressed-up men and women who knew Jamie Battle and had to greet him. He was open and backslapping with them, Black or white. A few of them were well-built, apparently single men, which made me wonder whether small town life might not be so bad after all. Jamie was definitely not inexperienced in bed.

At Beaulieu, we were greeted from the porch by barking dogs and Bill Barnes, sipping black coffee. "I was so drunk last night," he said to me. "I don't remember a thing." Jamie and I smiled at one another, and Bill Barnes frowned.

Everyone changed into more comfortable clothes, and some of the younger of us walked back across the road for another swim. This time, I watched Jamie Battle's body openly, and the cousins noticed, smiled, and whispered among themselves. While Jamie swam with them and I watched, Bill joined me on my towel, landing next to me with a thud.

"Had a good night then?" he asked, winking and leering at the same time. I pulled away. He gave me an innocent look. "What did I say?" he asked.

Back at the house, while the others rested or read or drank, Jamie Battle took me on a tour of some of his fields. It was his land, his house, and his life—although his father's family seemed always welcome to stay a while and reap some of the benefits.

"Do you see much of them?" I asked, while he gazed happily at a healthy expanse of cotton.

"More than y'all probably think," he answered. He looked me in the face. "They are good people, Henry. It's as strange for them as it is for me." Then, he changed the subject to cotton futures and we went on to another field. I asked who did the work; he couldn't possibly manage by himself.

"Mainly my farmhands," he said. "But I know how to plow and till." I was glad he didn't grin at the word *plow*. Suddenly eager, he asked, "Would you like to take a ride on a tractor?" I said I would.

Jamie trotted to a shed nearby, asking me to wait. In seconds, an engine burst into life inside the dark and, in seconds more, Jamie was backing out on a small John Deere. "Watch yourself," he warned as the tractor huffed and puffed backward toward me. I stepped aside as Jamie turned it toward the field. "Hop on," he said and pointed to where I could stand behind him. "Hold onto my shoulders," was his next instruction. I gripped them as gladly as I had the night before. "Ready?" he asked. I nodded. *I'm ready for anything*, I told only myself.

He positioned the tractor wheels precisely between the rows of soybeans, set the harrow down, and began to weed, gradually working his way across the field. I only know this because Jamie explained what he was doing as we trundled through the first rows.

The tractor jostled along, vibrating enough to make my brain rattle. The smell of gasoline and oil accompanied us. As the weeds fell under the machine, I could feel Jamie begin to sweat. "Why don't you stop?" I asked. He shut the engine off and looked around at me.

"You ready for a Coke-cola?" he asked.

"I'm ready for anything," I replied, out loud this time.

Jamie Battle's eyes widened and his mouth opened in a horse laugh I wouldn't have expected from him. But then, there was a lot I didn't know to expect from him.

"Well, come on then!" he said, restarting the tractor and heading down one last row.

At the end of it, he cut the motor and jumped off. I took his hand and stepped down more cautiously. Then, we ran for the trees parallel to the field and settled on the ground under a particularly large oak. His kisses were the sweetest ones I'd ever had.

Back at the house, only one of the cousins greeted us. "Everyone's gone to Rosedale or swimming," she said. She was in a bikini herself, golden-brown like the rest of them, except for Jamie Battle and me. Jamie and I went up to nap, deciding to make a declaration of some sort by sleeping together in his room. We were just drifting off when a knock came on the door.

"Jamie Battle?" Bill Barnes' voice asked.

"We're napping," he called.

"We?" Bill Barnes said, opening the door and walking into the room. Jamie yanked the bedspread over us and yelled at Bill Barnes to leave.

"Well, that answers one question," he said, grinning like a fool. "I was wondering where Henry Williams was." He shut the door behind him. "Look at the two of you. A mighty pretty combination, boys." He sat in the chair by the window, like he was going to watch.

"What else did you need, Bill?" Jamie Battle asked. He sounded irritated. That made two out of the three of us in the room.

Bill Barnes paid his irritation no mind. "Oh, yes. Y'all got me so distracted I almost forgot. Martha needs to ask you some questions about supper." Martha was the Beaulieu cook.

"I better see to this. It's about the party, I suppose," he said to me. To Bill, he said, "Thank you." Bill stared at us a few moments and then lurched up out of the chair.

"I best be going then," he said, laughing as he swaggered out of the room.

Jamie Battle pulled the spread off us and said, "Well, that cat is out of the bag."

"Do you care?"

"Not one bit," he answered solemnly.

I tried to kiss the seriousness off his face, but he pulled away.

"Now you save that for later," he said, trying to be stern, but he allowed me one more.

Monday morning, the day of the garden party, I woke up beside Jamie Battle again. He was still sleeping, his chest rising and falling with his breath. His ribcage showed its edges, and his flaccid brown cock sprawled across his groin. I reached out for it, feeling it swell.

"And good morning to you too," he said, stretching and rubbing his eyes with his knuckles. He pulled me into a kiss and an embrace. "It's going to be a busy day," he said, rubbing down my back to my ass and squeezing it familiarly.

"We should get up then," I told him, as he turned me around to spoon with him.

"Yes, we should," he agreed. "Eventually," he added, before rolling me onto my back.

Afterward, as I walked down the hall to my room, various members of the Barnes family greeted me as if it were the most natural thing in the world to see me strolling from Jamie Battle's room to mine in one of his robes. My own family would have been scandalized, for more than one reason.

Bill Barnes came into my room while I was buttoning my dress shirt. "Y'all like him then?" he asked before I could remind him to knock.

"I do," I answered, knotting a rep tie in a full Windsor.

He sat on my unused bed and then leaned across it, one arm akimbo. "I knew you would," he said, not looking very pleased about it.

"Is that why you invited me down here?" I asked, stuffing my shirttails inside my slacks.

"Not really," he answered, leaving it at that. He looked around the room, trying not to say something, I could tell. Finally, he lay back on the bed, hands behind his head. "I wasn't that drunk, you know," he said in a neutral tone.

"I suspected not," I told him as I sat next to him to pull on my socks and tie my shoes.

"I guess I blew it," he said, looking up at the ceiling like God might tell him otherwise. "I should have made my move earlier, in Memphis," he concluded.

"You weren't gay in Memphis," I reminded him, standing up.

He shifted to a sitting position, shiny tan shoes hitting the Persian rug. "I never should have said that," he told me. "I'm sorry I did, truly sorry." He shook his head. "I should never have brought you to Beaulieu," he mumbled, sounding bitter for the first time since I'd known him. "I know the kind of man Jamie Battle likes. What was I thinking?"

"Well, I'm glad you did," I said, tousling then recombing his wavy hair with my fingers. "Come on." I told him and yanked his unwilling body to its feet. "Let's go to this here garden party." I gave him a quick kiss on the cheek. He smiled ruefully.

"I guess you'll be back at Beaulieu pretty soon," he estimated.

"I certainly hope so," I said and pushed him toward the door. He laughed and opened it, letting me continue pushing him down the hall. By the time we reached the stairs, we were friends again and descended chatting as if nothing had changed between us in the last few days because, in the end, nothing had.

The French doors and their screens from the family parlor to the backyard were open wide, bugs be damned. People I didn't know greeted Bill Barnes and stared at me, smiling and curious, as we made our way through the house. Bill introduced me repeatedly as his *friend*, underlining, in my mind at least, what we might have been had we stayed in Memphis. But then we were through the gauntlet and finally outside. Jamie Battle came to join us. He looked so handsome in his tan suit, pale-blue shirt, and green patterned tie full of tiny pink roses. I dropped my hand from Bill's shoulder.

"Congratulations, cousin," Bill Barnes said sardonically.

Jamie smiled knowingly at him and took my hand.

"Let me introduce some folks to you, Henry," he said, his face sunny. I felt happy, too, mighty happy indeed. It was Labor Day at a sumptuous garden party outside an antebellum Southern mansion, tables piled high with food and drink, people chattering in a slow, Southern way, laughter rising and falling in waves across the lawn. Ladies and gentlemen in every shade of black, brown, and white wore gigantic hats and crisp summer suits. I waved at Mrs. Watts, seated with a coterie of other older women, all Black. The South had risen again at Beaulieu but probably not at all as some folks had predicted.

Jamie Battle looked about to burst with joy. I accepted a drink of something or other from a servant in suffocating black, and we walked hand in hand to meet his friends and neighbors.

They were certainly watching. What did they see? Two men holding hands? Someone white with someone Black? It didn't matter. I was ready. The party was on.

[This story was first published, in a slightly different form, in *Gay All Year*, short stories by the author published by NineStar Press.]

Día de los Muertos

Vincent Traughber Meis

The chair just inside the living room stuck out its leg as if it had agency and sent Marcus sprawling onto the floor, the vase he was carrying smashed, water creeping over the polished hardwood, and the marigolds just under his nose, tickling his nostrils with their pungent odor. He looked up into his father's stern face admonishing him from the framed photo. "Pay attention to what you're doing." He had heard it a thousand times.

The water reached the edge of the red Guatemalan tablecloth he had draped over the table, and it began to suck up the moisture, blotting along the hem and up the center, turning the cloth a deep crimson like a wound bleeding out. His hand throbbed, and he examined it, at first seeing nothing, and then a red line formed where a shard of glass had sliced the palm. Within seconds the line beaded and blood began to trickle across his palm and drip onto the orange marigolds that had been destined for the altar but were now fanned out on the floor, absorbing the drops of red.

He rose onto his knees and squeezed his hand with the other to stop the bleeding. From his kneeling position, he rose further to his feet and went to retrieve towels, one to wrap around his hand and the other to soak up the water on the floor.

In returning from the bathroom, he followed the trail of blood back to the altar, wrapping a thin towel around his hand and tucking it in. The other thicker one he dropped on the spreading water and stared into his father's blue eyes. Why had he chosen the serious photo of Henry even when his search had turned up several where he was smiling? "Dad, I'm such a klutz."

"No, you're not," said his mother from the photo of her at the beach in sunglasses and a wide-brimmed hat, occupying the other half of the altar. "You're like a gazelle when you run. And those hurdles! How do you do it?"

His father harrumphed. "Then he's paying attention."

When he was growing up, Marcus's parents often commented on his athletic ability on the field as opposed to his clumsiness at home. He was prone to accidents, tripping on stairs, hitting his head on open cabinets, letting the knife slip while helping his mom cook. When he was in middle school, he was called out of class by a counselor. The pleasant woman smiled a lot and asked if he often got in trouble at home. She assured him that everything he said was confidential and asked if he had been spanked as a child and how his parents punished him when he got in trouble.

"Is all this because of my black eye?" Marcus asked. He'd had a particularly bad week, tripping over his sneakers and literally run into a door, giving him the shiner, and then banging his head on a low hanging branch of the lemon tree.

"Your teachers say that you frequently have bruises."

"I'm super clumsy. Just ask my dad."

When the counselor became frustrated with that line of questioning, she took another avenue. "Do you ever feel like harming yourself?"

"What do you mean?"

"Some young people when they are feeling a lot of emotional pain cause themselves physical pain, which distracts them from what they are feeling."

"Like what?"

"Burn themselves in places where it won't be seen or cut themselves. Some even bang their heads against the wall."

"Seriously? Can I go back to class now?"

A few years later when his mom died, he entered a dark tunnel of anguish that seemed to have no end. One night he took a lighter and held it to his arm until the noxious smell of burning hair filled the air. He screamed and dropped the lighter. "What the fuck?" The pain in his heart was as bad as ever, and on top of that he had a burn on his arm that hurt like hell, and he'd have to hide it from his high school teachers.

He swept up the broken glass of the vase and found a plastic one for the blood-stained marigolds, which he placed next to his dad's tattered and sweat-stained San Francisco Giants baseball cap and his mom's fingerless gloves she had worn around the house from October to April, complaining that she could never get her hands warm. He got a whiff of his mom's favorite Salvadorean cornbread with sesame seeds on top he had just picked up from the bakery that afternoon and rotated the bottle of his dad's favorite beer so he could see the Rolling Rock label. Seashells they had found at the beach in Mexico on trips to see his grandparents were scattered around the altar. He picked up a dog collar and moved it closer to the photo of their beloved dog, Charlie, who used to keep his mom company when she was sick and then passed a few months after she did. It was the first Día de los Muertos the ofrenda was dedicated to the three of them, Marta, Henry and Charlie. He was slowly getting used to being alone with no family to call his own or a special person in his life. Yes, he had a few friends, he reminded himself, friends who would be arriving soon for his annual face-painting party before the Día de los Muertos procession through his neighborhood in the Mission District. This would be the first year his father wouldn't be joining them. The previous year Henry had been so full of life, hugging everyone at the end of the night and sleeping on the couch in the living room because he'd had one too many beers.

He made a few last-minute adjustments, rearranging the flowers so they weren't blocking any of the photos and spreading the lemons from his father's tree in Visitation Valley around the altar. He had gone by the house earlier in the day, the house where he grew up and where his father had a heart attack at the age of forty-seven. He picked a few lemons from the tree but avoided going inside.

He was startled by his father's voice, saying, "You need someone in your life. I thought you and..."

"I'm not going to have this conversation. Not now. I can't."

His father's expression turned from stern to disappointed. His mom stayed silent. He lit a votive candle that cast a warm light on her face, her brown eyes and hair that he'd inherited. He looked into her eyes and saw his own face superimposed on hers, a trick of the glass in the frame. He lit several more candles and the altar came alive, an ofrenda to the dead coming alive. He smiled at the joke. The flames grew and he was captivated by the colors, the flickering, the dancing shadows of the marigolds. It started to happen, the absence, his momentary vacation from the merry-go-round of the earth. His world became suspended, frozen, the sounds and sights locked out just beyond his perimeter. His line of sight was limited to the yellow-orange flame and it calmed him, making him want to stay in the absence forever.

"Marcus!" shouted his father. But the sound was so very faint it might have been the buzz of an insect in the next county.

The absence first happened after his mother died. It took away the pain at least for a moment or two. His eyelids fluttered around his eyes sending out beams of golden light and his lips smacked as if anticipating the Salvadorean cornbread. As it always happened, something would break through, a sound, a smell, a change in light. This time it was the musty odor of marigolds that cork-screwed up his nose like a bee and shook him from his trance.

As he came back to the room, the altar, the marigolds tinged with red, and night falling outside the windows, he became aware of a pounding at the door that had reached a level indicating it had been going on for some time. Marcus took one slow step, and then another like an engine that need to warm up. With his head still foggy, the hallway seemed never-ending, but he eventually reached the front door and opened it.

"Thank God, Marcus! I have to pee so bad." Ash held a hand pressed below the waist of her long flower-embroidered huipil she had gotten in Oaxaca the summer before. She pushed by him and ran to the bathroom.

Jane shrugged and straightened her black beret that hid her spikey blond hair. She wore a black suit, black shiny shirt, and black tie. "Oh my God, Marcus! What happened?" She pointed at the blood seeping through the towel around his hand.

"What the fuck?" Ash yelled from the bathroom. "Was there a murder up in here?"

The three of them reunited in the dining room where the plastic draped table was covered with face paint, brushes, make-up sponges, mirrors, pencils, sequins, more marigolds, and a large bag of plastic spiders.

"Honey, what happened?" said Ash.

"I was carrying a vase of flowers to the altar and tripped."

Jane took ahold of his arm and turned it over. She scrunched her face and looked away. "Sorry. I'm no nurse Nancy."

"Me neither," said Ash. "Sergio will be here soon. He'll know what to do. In the meantime, give me a hug." Marcus hugged Ash and then Jane, holding his injured hand out from his body so as not to smear them with blood.

"Does it hurt?" said Jane while adjusting the crown of marigolds in Ash's thick curls that had gotten knocked off kilter in the hug.

"Like a son of a bitch."

A knock on the door made Ash's eyebrows jump. "I hope that's Sergio and co," she said. "That shit's giving me the woozers." The towel was now more red than white. "I'll get the door."

A minute later Ash dragged Sergio into the room, followed by Josh, Fer, and Pats. "Hey, Serge," said Marcus, holding up his arm. "I need you. Sorry."

Sergio's face opened like he had waited his whole life to hear those words. He took Marcus by the arm and lead him toward the bathroom. Over his shoulder, Marcus said, "Libations and snackeries in the kitchen. Have at it, lushes."

Sergio and Marcus disappeared into the bathroom.

"Maybe they'll finally hook up," said Jane.

"Yeah, if we lock them in there for ten years," said Josh.

"Give Marcus a break," said Pats. "His dad just died."

"The only man he ever loved," said Jane. They all went owl-eyed like she'd trashed RuPaul's Drag Race or said she'd voted Republican.

"Fuck, Jane," said Fer. "Uncalled for. A little respect?"

"What do you know about respect?" He shook his head and started toward the kitchen with the six-pack he had brought. "Let's get dranks."

"I'm a tequila girl tonight," said Ash. "You bitches are starting already." Fer and Jane had gone out together before he hooked up with Josh. Bitters lingered.

Marcus and Sergio emerged from the bathroom to half-painted faces and the sweet aroma of weed in the air. A truce had been called so they could focus on putting on their dead faces. Someone had tuned in The Doors on Spotify. "Love Her Madly" was playing.

"Did you kiss it and make it better?" said Jane.

"No," said Marcus. "He sucked my blood and now we're both vampires."

Fer wobbled his head at Jane and guffawed.

"Somebody's going to have to do me," said Marcus.

"I will," said Sergio.

"It's about time," said Josh.

"You're all whacked," said Pats.

"Sit down over here, Marcus," said Ash as she attached sequins around her eyes. "We can both work on you. I'm almost finished."

"Did everyone see the ofrenda in the living room?" said Marcus.

"Loved the blood-splattered marigolds," said Josh. "Congrats on the creepy feels."

"It was an accident. Who would plan something like that?"

"I miss Henry," said Pats. "This is the first year without him."

Everyone nodded and they launched into stories about different years he had joined them for Day of the Dead, like the year it was unseasonably warm and he went shirtless with his rocking forty-something body painted like a skeleton or the time he ate too many brownies, not realizing they were fortified and face-planted on the grass in the park, coming within inches of destroying one of the altars.

Marcus's parents were teenagers when Marta got pregnant, making Henry only seventeen years older than Marcus, a gap that became less significant as the years went by. At times Marcus enjoyed having his father as a friend, but sometimes he just wanted him to be his dad. Henry never missed a Day of the Dead and he occasionally partied with Marcus's friends at other gatherings, wilding out with the best of them while Marcus, who didn't drink or smoke, would silently observe from the sofa how his dad fit in better with his friends than he did. When dancing was in the mix, Henry was the first on the floor; Marcus never danced. Both his gay and straight friends frequently commented on how hot his dad was, especially when they realized how much it annoyed Marcus.

It was no secret that Pats had a crush on Henry, but the group of friends was surprisingly quiet about it. At a New Year's Eve party a couple of years before, Marcus had stepped into the cold on the back porch and caught Pats and his dad making out, adding another layer of shiver onto his already chilly mood. His face stretched in two directions, his jaw falling and his eyes jumping up. He tried to discreetly return to the kitchen but tripped on the sill of the doorway, bumping his head on the door and generally causing a ruckus. Lips unlocked, followed by a groan from Henry.

"Why don't you hang out with your own friends?" Marcus said angrily when all the guests had left.

"Because my friends are boring," Henry said, unable to fully open his eyes, his grin unstoppable, his stance wobbly.

"Your stay-youthful plan by partying with thirty-year-olds is so annoying."

Henry hung his head but didn't seem remorseful in the least. "Your mom's been gone fifteen years now."

"It's not about that!" shouted Marcus. "Pats is my friend. Hitting on her is so lame."

Henry cough-chuckled. "You assume I hit on her."

"Stop. I can't."

In front of his apartment building on 25th Street, they took a group pic to add to the photo collection of ghoulish white faces, cavernous eye sockets, exaggerated painted-on teeth, documenting the changing expertise in face painting over the last ten years, and the emerging fashions that enhanced the look of death. Ash took a video for her YouTube channel, and Josh snapped a ton of selfies to update his story on Instagram. It was all so public, and the same cadre of Instagrammers and Tiktokers and Twitter sluts would click on hearts and the comments would be predictable. A few days later everyone would have moved on to the next thing. Marcus loved his friends but sometimes needed a break from their unrelenting obsession to be unique and relevant and seen. He could go weeks without looking at social media. He went to his job at Airbnb as leader of the App Innovations Team, came home, fixed dinner, and watched TV or sometimes read. He wasn't constantly out on the streets or in bars or in restaurants. That's why he hosted parties. To see his friends. And when the party was over, he was already home. The cleanup was a small price to pay for the convenience of having his friends come to him.

The procession had already started on 24th Street. Marcus and his friends fell in behind the Batalá drumming group all dressed in white unlike most of the people on the street who wore black. For Marcus, the regular pounding on the skin of the drums had a soothing effect. Within minutes he felt calmer, his anxieties not being able to stand up to the beat that went right to his solar plexus, the rhythmic core where humans remembered their mothers' heartbeats. The grief of losing his parents became instead a shield of his parents' love protecting him; the angst he often felt in the presence of his friends turned into a web of connectedness as they danced along by his side; his dwelling in the past about his father's involvement with his friends changed to an admiration for Henry's youthful spirit; and his discomfort about not being capable of returning Sergio affection dissipated, allowing him to throw an arm over Serge's shoulder and draw him closer. He loved Sergio in his way but not *that* way. With each drumbeat, his blood pressure lowered, and his stress melted.

After his mother's death when he was fifteen, his father bought him a drum set. It sat in the corner for days until one afternoon he picked up the sticks and started pounding. He drummed until his hands were numb, but it felt good, the pain in his heart not forgotten but softened. So much better than his experiment with the lighter. For the next two years, he practiced drumming every day, causing the neighbors to complain and his father to build him a soundproof room in the garage.

He released Sergio and started to move his body to the drumming like the others, awkwardly at first, drawing stares. A minute later he began spinning, imitating some of the dancers accompanying the drummers. As he spun, he saw multiple Catrinas, the mother icon of skeletons, faces painted like skulls and wearing embroidered tunics or blouses and elaborate flowered hats or intricate hair designs with marigolds woven through them. Children, too, looked like mini cadavers, marching with their parents who introduced them at an early age to the notion that death wasn't necessarily something to fear. Even a black Labrador's coat had been painted to look like a skeleton dog.

Marcus bumped into a giant cardboard Catrina and would have fallen if the person carrying the Catrina hadn't grabbed his arm. He stopped spinning and the light from hand-held candles and the din of the crowd receded as he found himself at the edge of the procession, his friends no longer in sight, the drums distant, and his anxieties returning, seeping like black oil into his brain. His hand throbbed. He ducked into an alley between 24th and 25th Streets where most of the garages were painted with murals. The normally busy alley because of its artwork was surprisingly quiet when he reached the middle, looking to the end one way to see crowds passing by in one direction, and at the opposite end, crowds passing in the other direction. He sat on the ground and leaned against a garage door mural with an assembly of indigenous women holding their fists in the air above his head. He closed his eyes and let his forehead fall onto his knees. The drums were now muted thuds, barely discernible, drowned out by his own pounding heart. He took deep breaths.

"Are you okay?" said a tenuous voice.

Marcus opened his eyes on a tall thin man about his age. The first thing he noticed was his ice-blue eyes like his father's, and a chill ripped through him. He was dressed casually in a white hoodie and sweats. His white kicks looked fresh from the box. His face was pale but not made up, and a few black curls tumbled onto his forehead.

"I'm fine."

The man nodded with a grin. "As in fucked-up, insecure, neurotic, and emotional."

"What?"

"Isn't the answer 'fine' most of the time just an acronym for what you're really feeling?"

"Look, I don't know what your thing is, but you know nothing about me."

"Maybe you should tell me. Can I sit?"

"No, you can't. I need some alone time."

The young man ignored his rejection and in an instant was sitting next to Marcus. "I'll just sit quietly. You won't even know I'm here."

Marcus started to get up, but the visitor touched his arm. "Please. Maybe I'm the one that's F-I-N-E."

The man's touch sent a white-hot liquid through him, leaving him immobile, paralyzed. At first his heart began to race, but after a few seconds of the hand on his arm, the pounding slowed until his heart barely beat at all. His breathing slowed.

"Better?" said the stranger. His voice was like a whisper that could be heard blocks away.

Marcus nodded, avoiding the man's eyes, afraid to look at him.

"I'm Zeke."

"Hey. Marcus here."

"If you're okay now, I can go." He released his arm.

With the contact gone, Marcus felt an unsettling emptiness. "Sorry. I was rude. You can stay."

Zeke settled in, leaned back, and took Marcus's bandaged hand in his. "What happened?"

Marcus flinched.

"Are my hands cold?"

"Like ice."

"I can never get them warm."

"Like my mom. She used to wear those fingerless gloves all the time." Marcus looked down at his hand where blood seeped through the bandage. "I guess my being fucked-up, insecure, neurotic, and emotional led to the accident." They both chuckled.

"Shit happens," said Zeke.

They sat quietly. A few people passed by like ghosts, not even glancing at them.

"It's not easy to be alone in the world." Zeke's voice was still like a deep whisper.

"What the… ?"

"You've lost both your mom and dad, right?"

"No!" He lied, feeling emotionally violated, as if being probed by aliens after an abduction. "You're wrong. They're fi... they're okay."

"That's good." Zeke fell silent, a silence that was louder than when he spoke.

"What are you doing here?"

"I noticed you and felt a deep sadness."

"Noticed me? Where?"

"On the street. You were whirling like a dervish."

"So, you followed me?"

"I'm not trying to upset you. I felt a pull. It's hard to explain."

Zeke's voice soothed him even though he wanted so badly to be angry at Zeke, at the world. The ground was hard and cold. He sniffled and wiped his nose. He chanced a look at Zeke, and the eyes no longer frightened him. Zeke's face was smooth, cheekbones pushing against milky skin, a fine nose resting above thin but inviting lips. He had a peculiar desire to kiss him. The desire to kiss anyone was rare. How many times had he gazed at Sergio who had the most beautiful full lips of any man he'd ever met, and yet he couldn't imagine kissing him? Zeke smiled and seemed to know what he was thinking.

Marcus looked away to hide his eyes.

"Feeling something, huh?" said Zeke.

"I got some dust in my eyes."

"You were thinking of kissing me."

Marcus shook his head. "That's absurd. I barely know you."

"Are you sure about that?"

"What? Like we met in a previous lifetime in ancient Egypt or something?"

"Maybe lots of times."

Marcus again had the urge to get up and run away. He was too close to something he didn't understand, too close to losing control.

But the presence of Zeke continued to slow down of his heart and quiet his breathing, acting like a lazy truth serum, making him ready to tell Zeke everything. A tear ran down his cheek. What was happening to him? "What if I did think about it?"

"What's stopping you?"

"About a million things." He ran his sleeve under his nose. "I've got a runny nose. I think I'm coming down with a cold."

"No. You're just F-I-N-E. Especially the last one, emotional."

"Are you playing with me?"

"That is not something I would ever do. You are too important to me."

"In ten minutes, I'm important to you?"

"You're forgetting those other lifetimes."

"You're wicked weird." He sniffled.

"You don't know the half of it."

Marcus's tears were unstoppable now, and the sniffling had gotten worse. He covered his face with his uninjured hand. Zeke put an arm around him and pulled him close. Marcus couldn't remember the last time someone had held him like that, not like a friend, not like a father, like someone who wanted to merge with him. He opened his eyes and looked up. This time there was no choice. Their lips fit together like parts of a puzzle. Zeke's mouth tasted of menthol that went straight to his brain, a soothing balm. Their tongues played a game of tag. The outside world was suspended like in his absences, but this time there were two of them like two pillars of smoke twisted around each other, rising up and away from the earth. The feeling of being away was so strong, he began to fear he would never come back, and part of him didn't care.

Fireworks sounded nearby and Marcus jumped, pulled back. In the streetlight he saw Zeke's perfect face was smudged with his black and white makeup as if his dead face was trying to transfer to Zeke's. Marcus tried to rub it off with his thumb, remembering how his mother used to do it when she kissed him wearing lipstick.

"Don't worry about it," Zeke said, stopping the rubbing by taking Marcus's hand in his.

Marcus sighed. "I don't kiss a lot of people."

"Me neither. Nobody these days." He rested his hand on Marcus's chest. "Your heart is at full gallop."

"And yours?" Marcus lifted his hand to touch Zeke's chest, but Zeke gently took hold of his wrist and moved his hand back around his waist. "You're beating for both of us." Zeke kissed him again. Marcus was ready to go all in, be taken away, meld with Zeke's coolness, but Zeke broke off the kiss and rested his chin on Marcus's shoulder.

"Do you live near here?" Marcus asked. He didn't mean it to sound like a lead-in to being invited over. He was thinking ahead, wondering how they would get together again.

"Not anymore. My parents still live in the neighborhood."

The invasion of other voices came into Marcus's head, people coming down the alley from both directions. The procession must have ended, and the flow of bodies filled the narrow street.

"Marcus," a voice rang out.

Marcus jumped up, awkward and shaken like the time he had startled his dad and Pats kissing. Guilt spread over him as he stood in front of Sergio, wondering if he had seen him kissing Zeke.

Beyond Sergio were his other friends, and he moved toward them.

"We've been looking all over for you," said Pats.

"I just needed a little break from all the noise."

"What were you doing sitting on the ground?" asked Sergio.

Marcus whirled around. Zeke was no longer there. "Hold on a sec."

He hurried back to where they had been sitting and then down the alley, his heart thumping wildly, weaving in and out of people. "Zeke!" he shouted. "Zeke!"

As each step brought him closer to the end of the alley, a sinking feeling weighed down his legs. His friends caught up with him.

"What's going on?" said Fer.

"Have you been crying?" said Jane.

"Oh, God, your hand is bleeding," said Sergio. "I told you you needed stitches."

Their voices, though well meaning, grated on his nerves.

Pats put her arm around him. “Honey, we're worried about you. What can we do?”

Marcus trembled with the notion that Zeke hadn't really existed, that he had conjured him up in the absence and tried to bring him back to the real world. The best kiss of his life, the first time he felt a true connection with another person might have just been a dream. “Did you see someone sitting next to me?”

“Someone sitting next to you?” Pats shook her head.

“You met someone?” said Josh.

“I didn't see anyone,” said Ash.

Jane shrugged with a worried look on her face.

Marcus looked at each one of them. “Nobody?”

A stranger bumped into Marcus and he spun around, expecting to see Zeke's cool blue eyes. The person in a long black coat and a scary mask staggered. “Watch where you're going, asshole,” Marcus said.

“Fuck you,” the man mumbled.

In a stance his friends had never witnessed, Marcus puffed out his chest and balled his fists.

Josh grabbed Marcus and pulled him away from the drunk while his friends all stared in shock at this new manifestation of Marcus.

Sergio chewed his lower lip. “I saw someone.” His voice was tinged with hurt. “In a white hoodie.”

“Yes!” Joy coursed through him. He wasn't crazy. Zeke was real. He couldn't have gone far. “But why would he run away?”

“Maybe we scared him,” said Fer.

“We?” said Jane. “It was probably you.”

Marcus ignored them and pointed toward Garfield Square with hope blossoming on his face. He stood on tiptoes and craned his neck toward the crowds gathering in the park across the street. “Let's go look at the altars. Maybe he's there.”

Multiple ofrendas had been set up in the small park, some large with multiple levels and tons of candles, photos of various family members, and every inch of the tables covered with bouquets of flowers, trinkets, and favorite foods of the deceased. Others were simple altars of a card table covered with a cloth dedicated to one person. A lot of the marchers in the procession now wandered the park, paying their respects, looking for friends. Marcus and his group walked past a troop of flamenco dancers, their heels clacking on a wooden stage, their faces made up like skulls, the high-pitched voices and frantic guitar playing sending out a message of anguish and despair. The Batalá drummers had assembled in one corner of the square, joined by others with cowbells, tambourines, maracas, and gongs. Smoke spiraled into the air from fire pits, candles, people smoking cigarettes and joints. It was tribal and rhythmic with most people's true identities hidden by masks and makeup and adorned in attire fit for burial. It was a diorama representing a world between life and death.

Marcus swiveled his neck and strained his eyes burning from the smoke, searching, feeling confident that Zeke would be easy to spot, his tall frame in gleaming white clothes and face without makeup. Sergio remained by his side, eyes downcast, and the others followed, sometimes stopping to gawk at a photo of someone who had gone to the other side or make a comment of sympathy to a family member who stood by the altar.

With his eyes peeled for whiteness, Marcus was drawn to a small table, barely larger than a bedside table, covered with a white sheet, behind which a middle-aged couple, also dressed in white, sat on plastic chairs. The altar contained a single votive candle and a framed photo. The woman gazed at Marcus and then a smile emerged delicately as if struggling with the sadness on the rest of her face. There was something familiar about her smile.

Sergio took Marcus's arm. "I still think we should get you some stitches. St. Luke's is just a few blocks away."

Marcus shook his arm out of Sergio's grip. He stared now at the man with cool blue eyes who sat next to the woman. Then his eyes fell to the photo, the image flickering in the candlelight. He took a step closer, his heart pounding, his mouth parched. He leaned closer still. In the picture was a young man in a white hoodie and white sweats, the face of an angel. Marcus pointed a shaky finger at the photograph. "His… his name?" he croaked.

"That is our son, Zeke," said the man.

"He's…" Marcus felt his throat lock.

"With the angels now," said the woman.

Marcus's legs buckled. Sergio caught him before he hit the ground. Ash, Jane, and Pats rushed forward to help.

"No, no, no, no…" Marcus hit his injured hand against his forehead. The blood spot on his bandage grew.

The couple stood up, their faces confused, lips twisted, as if the pain of their son's death had been released again from their weary hearts. "Did you know our son?" the man asked.

"Marcus, stop," whispered Sergio. "You're upsetting these nice people."

"It was him," said Marcus in a distant voice. "I kissed him."

Marcus's friends led him away, Sergio on one side and Ash on the other.

"He's had a difficult day," Pats said to the couple. "He lost his father recently."

Marcus planted his feet, struggled, and broke away from Sergio and Ash. He approached the couple who had returned to their seats and fell to his knees beside the woman's chair. "Yes. I knew him. A short time, but I will never forget it. When did he…?"

The woman looked down at the folded hands in her lap. "Three months ago. On his birthday. My husband took the photo that day." She pointed at the frame. "He wanted to do a bay swim to celebrate his twenty-fifth birthday. He was a good swimmer."

Marcus could still feel Zeke's chilly touch on his skin, his cool lips, like dry ice, hot and cold, burning his soul and calming his heart. "I'm sorry." He bowed his head, oblivious to the impossibility of the meeting, knowing it was as real as anything that had happened to him recently.

Zeke's mother leaned forward and spoke softly in his ear. "He visits me, too."

Marcus nodded. "That gives me hope."

She lay a hand on the top of his head as if giving him a blessing. "Go in peace, my son."

Marcus stood up and backed away. His friends circled him in a protective huddle.

"At least let me re-bandage your hand," said Sergio. "We'll walk you home."

Marcus passed the next hour in a daze, letting them take care of him, trying to act normal despite a new persona taking over from the inside. With a fresh bandage on his hand, his face scrubbed of paint, the mess in the dining room cleaned up by Fer and Pats, Marcus convinced his friends they should leave. Their worried faces lost some of their edge. "I'm fine," he said with a silly grin.

Alone he crawled into bed, but not alone like before. The hope of the next meeting glowed inside him, warming and cooling at the same time. He closed his eyes and put his chilly fingers to his lips. Remembering. Hoping. Waiting.

Thanksgiving Pie

M.D. Neu

Things happen all around us to be thankful for; always be grateful and open to something or someone new.

David felt a pang of loneliness as he walked up McKee Road, the route much too busy for today of all days, but people always had last-minute shopping to finish, or places to be and friends and family to get to. Also, not everyone celebrated today, but most people did. After all, this wasn't a religious holiday; today was a secular event. He glanced towards the cloudy grey sky matching his mood.

Why won't it rain already and stop torturing us.

San Jose should be sunny, not cloudy, but with the weather changing who really knew anymore. He relocated to San Jose, specifically the Alum Rock area, six months ago for a new job in IT, after losing the best CIS job he ever had. His last employer had been his first real job and the one he had started at while still in college. The loss was the first massive thorn in his side, to be followed by many more, leaving him battered and bruised.

Adding more spikes, David hadn't made any real friends yet. Well, not like the friends he had back home, folks he could call and meet up with in a heartbeat, if he wanted to be around people and not feel lonely. Sure, there were some work friends, but not people he wanted to hang out with all the time. Making matters pricklier, his family lived in Salt Lake City, and he couldn't afford to fly back this year for Thanksgiving, especially on such short notice, adding to his gloom. Also off the list were his friends from college who were all scattered around the country, and his boyfriend had dumped him two weeks ago for someone else.

"The fucker," he whispered under his breath as he continued into the parking lot, the scents of petrol and exhaust assaulting his nose.

He hated spending holidays alone. At least he already had the tickets for Christmas; not seeing everyone at Christmas would be too much to bear. He missed the warmth and laughter of his family and friends, the smell of his mom's cooking, the homemade rolls, the mashed potatoes with real cream, and the pies—*oh those wonderful pumpkin and berry pies*—the sound of his dad's jokes, the same ones he told every year since childhood. His brother-in-law,

Chad, cheerfully yelling at his kids, David's nieces and nephews, to be quiet or to get out of the way so he could enjoy the football game, at least until the clock ran out, ending the game. Then Chad would insist that they all go out and play touch football. David shuddered at the memory of playing football–one thing he wouldn't miss.

His sister Lisa married the perfect guy, because of course she did. Her husband's only fault is his obsession with football, but was football really a fault or more of an annoyance? David shrugged. Another sigh escaped his mouth as he dodged someone pulling into one of the parking spaces. At least the blond guy with the goatee offered him a slight wave as an apology, while the dark-haired guy next to him shook his head. He wished he had someone special in his life. Relationships continued to be a nightmare, especially for a gay man in his 30s who wanted more than a one-and-done. He wanted someone who cared about him and loved him, like his parents and his sister had. Why were relationships so difficult? And dating wasn't made any easier when a lot of the queer community believed that once you hit 30 you might as well not exist.

Why are relationships so hard to find?

He thought he had found the right guy, but…

David pushed the thought from his head. He didn't want to give that asshole any more space in his mind than he already had.

No more living in my brain rent free... bastard.

Watching the glass doors slide apart as he entered the inside of the busy store, with a basket in hand, synthetic holiday music already playing, David made his way past the fresh fruits and vegetables, bypassing them for the chiller. Snatching a bag-o-salad and tossing the package into his basket, he made his way to the back where the bakery usually overflowed with cookies, cakes, breads, rolls, and other sweet delights, clearly now picked over. David didn't find anything tasty; seemingly all the good pies were already gone.

"Oh sure." He shook his head and moved on, weaving between the other shoppers rushing about. At least no one would run into him with their shopping cart.

"Ouch!" David yelped, the heavy plastic hitting his heels and causing him to move over and stumble.

"Oh, I'm sorry," a kid, couldn't be more then seventeen, said from behind his phone, before rushing off.

David closed his eyes and took a deep breath, trying to keep from exploding. He pushed his annoyance as far down as it would go as he continued on to the freezer section at the other end of the store.

Let's get what I need and get the hell out of here.

Glaring at the glass door, he searched for a crappy frozen turkey and mashed potatoes dinner from what appeared to be a much too large selection of other crappy frozen dinners, hoping to make himself a decent meal somewhat resembling a Thanksgiving dinner. He knew his supper wouldn't compare to the real thing—nothing ever did—but a frozen dinner would be better than nothing. And he really didn't want to spend the time, money or effort on creating a big meal for himself. Plus, *they* were supposed to do Thanksgiving Dinner tonight together over at his ex's house. His ex had promised to make him the best meal he ever had, but not now. A knot tightened in his stomach as his hand clenched together. He glowered at the bag-o-salad in his basket. How much more miserable could this day get? And how much more depressed could he become? Muzak echoed throughout the entire store, casting his surroundings in happy artificial noises that David had no interest in focusing on. He was busy checking out the different lonely heart meals that mocked him from behind the glass barrier.

Can this be any more disappointing?

Pulling open the glass door, instantly slapped by a blast of cold air that caused the door to fog up, he grabbed the frozen dinner that appeared the least offensive to his senses and dropped the frozen box into his basket next to the basic bag of green salad laying there, no longer lonely like him. With an inhale, he decided he had everything he needed for his grand feast for one.

Except for dessert, but who cares.

Stepping back, David didn't notice the guy who bumped into him until he heard a loud thud and watched his basket and groceries cascade into the aisle in front of him. "God dammit!" He looked up and saw a handsome stranger, holding a pumpkin pie in his hands. A look of shock and a slight frown started filling his face. The pale-yellow button-down shirt underneath a tan light-weight jacket framed his strong shoulders, showing off a firm neck. His chiseled chin dusted with impeccably sculpted stubble enhanced his full lips, brown eyes, and shaved head. His handsome features did nothing to keep David's exasperation from building.

"Hey, I'm so sorry, I didn't see you there." The man kneeled down to help David pick up his things. "Are you okay?"

The frustration in David, no longer happily contained deep down, boiled to a surge of anger. The final straw broke his proverbial back. He had been looking forward to eating that turkey dinner, frozen mess and all. Sure, the meal would be overly salted and overly processed crap, but what wasn't crap in his life these days. And now his dinner lay ruined. The box bent, which meant the interior tray would be messed up and who knows what condition the contents would be in now. Would the meal be ruined? No. Was he being ridiculous? Probably, but that's what anger did; it screwed up your thought process. He faced the man and snapped, not caring if he was being rude or who heard.

"Yeah, I'm fine, no thanks to you." The venom poured from his lips as he snatched his basket from the man's hand. "Just watch where you're going next time. I suppose I should be happy you're not running people over with a shopping cart."

Confusion and hurt filled the handsome man's face, any sparkle in his eyes vanishing. The guy's friendly smile faltered, although he still seemed genuinely apologetic. But David didn't care. Since he moved here everything had turned to shit. Today sucked, but it wasn't just today; he had been having a bad month and a bad year. Today he just wanted to get his crappy meal, go home and wallow in self-pity. And now, David added to that list. He wanted someone else to suffer as much as he was hurting at the moment. He didn't care if his actions were right or wrong; he wasn't going to be the only one anguishing anymore.

This whole move had been a mistake. I should have stayed back in Utah.

"I said I was sorry, what's your problem?" the man bit back as he took a step backward, then opened his mouth and closed it, not saying any more.

David sighed and rubbed his forehead as he stood. Annoying cheerful holiday music made its way to his ears, terrorizing him. Okay, yes, his current actions were unfair. Yes, his emotions were probably a bit out of control at the moment, but he couldn't help how he felt. He was lonely and bummed out. So much had happened in such a short time that he suspected the universe was out to get him. And having this man plow into him pushed David over the edge. Pity and rage filled every corner of him, and David wanted—no, needed—someone to blame, and this poor guy stood in the line of fire. This man simply ended up in the wrong place at the wrong time.

"My problem is that I'm alone on Thanksgiving, and I have nothing to be thankful for," he blurted out, not able to keep his mouth closed. "My boyfriend dumped me, my friends are all over the country, my parents and the rest of my family are back in Utah, and I'm here alone and…" He waved his hand around. "This stupid store and the lousy fake music, and…" He took a breath, trying to calm down. He refused to burst into tears over all this stupidness, especially here in a grocery store in front of this majorly hot guy. "I'm sorry. You didn't… You… I'm sorry." David shook his head as heat rose up his neck and warmed his cheeks, making a final stop in his temples.

The man's expression softened. A smile bloomed across his lips, showing off his straight white teeth as he offered his hand to David. "Hi, I'm Fernando," he beamed, the sparkle returning and brightening his eyes. "And I think you do have at least one thing to be thankful for."

David glanced at his frozen dinner and salad in his basket, then back to Fernando skeptically. What could he possibly have to be thankful for? His life sucked.

"What's that?" he tried to keep his tone in check and remembered this guy wasn't his ex. "The bad music or all the people rushing about with places to go… except… ugh, sorry." He pursed his lips and took another deep breath. He held the air in his lungs a bit longer before releasing, and that helped calm him down.

Fernando pointed at the pumpkin pie. "This." He held up the pie, beaming. "It's the last one they had in the bakery, and it's delicious. I noticed you looking at the pies and since you didn't grab one, I thought you might be looking for pumpkin. How about you come with me to my place and we share it? I can assure you what I have at home for dinner is going to be a lot better than that boxed meal you have in your basket."

"Wait." David stopped and glanced at the man up and down. "You followed me?"

Fernando's cheeks pinkened and he bit at his bottom lip. "Well, no. I mean." Now Fernando stumbled over his words. "You seemed upset… but, you know, I thought you were cute." He cleared his throat. "Anyway, I just picked up the pie and I wanted to… um… meet you."

"You followed me through the store." David's tone now more amused than anything. Here he was feeling sorry for himself, sulking through the store, and all the while this guy followed him while trying to manufacture a way to meet and talk.

And here we are.

Fernando ran his free hand over his shaved head and glanced around the aisle. "That about sums it up." His eyes opened wider as they filled with hope dusted with embarrassment. "What do you say? Care to share…?" He held up the pie.

David hesitated. He didn't know this guy, this Fernando person, and he wasn't sure if the universe wasn't still trying to play some kind of cruel joke and send him another jerk to mess with him. But he had to admit the offer intrigued him. Fernando definitely held high marks on the scale for looks and he had a warm charm about him. He also smelled amazing. David wasn't sure of the scent but the cologne caused him to inhale again. And a big plus, at least for David, was that this guy seemed to have a pretty decent sense of humor, unlike old what's-his-name. All positives in David's book. He peeked at his frozen dinner that was reminding him he didn't have anything better to do. David supposed if the guy happened to be a serial killer or something worse, he wouldn't be making this offer in a grocery store full of witnesses.

"Oh, I don't…" David shook his head. "I mean, I appreciate the offer." Should he do this? A big part of him wanted to say yes. Still, going back with this hottie to his place for pie and who knows what else might not be a good idea.

But then again.

"I understand." The vivacity dimmed in Fernando's eyes. "For all you know, I'm some crazy pumpkin pie serial killer." He managed to smirk with a laugh and hints of fire, or passion, still peeking out.

"Well, are you?" David couldn't help but smile as his lips twisted up on his face.

Fernando continued to laugh, then took a breath. "Whatever answer I give you could be a lie. So, I guess the only way to find out would be to join me. I can assure you the pie'll be worth it."

David thought a moment. What did he really have to lose? Yes, the guy could kill him, but he didn't think so. David had a pretty good sense about these things, and somehow the fact that Fernando made a joke of being a murderer suggested he wasn't a killer.

I hope. And really, what's the difference between meeting this guy here or at the bar or using one of the many hookup apps out there?

"Give me your phone." Fernando looked at the pie. "I'll trade you."

David snickered and pulled out his phone, opened the device to his contacts, then took the pie from Fernando.

Fernando tapped away, then held the phone up and took a picture. "Here's my address, name and phone number. Text it to someone you trust and let them know what you're doing and ask them to contact you later tonight to check in."

"Seriously?" David couldn't believe this guy. Was he for real? He took back his phone as Fernando took the pie. "I mean, I could send a note to my sister…" He shrugged.

"That works," Fernando offered with a bright smile. "Anyway, it's Thanksgiving, and I can't stand the idea of you being alone after a breakup." Hints of pink danced around his cheeks. "We've all been there and it sucks."

David nodded and tapped away, sending a message to Lisa, his sister, letting her know to message him in a couple of hours.

"Are we good?" Fernando asked, adjusting the pie in his hands.

"How do you know I'm not a murderer?" David glanced at the pie. Well, the dessert did look good, and the man definitely was easy on his eyes. "Or just interested in your pie?"

“I don’t.” Fernando glanced at the people around them. “But I also don’t think so. You don’t fit the profile.”

“Profile… what are you, a cop or something?”

“San Jose PD, five years now.” Fernando pulled out his badge and wallet to show David.

All David could do was laugh. This was too much. He just met a handsome cop in a grocery store who’s offering to share his Thanksgiving meal with him. “Okay, we can go back to your place, but I walked here. I live over on Toyon.” He slipped his phone in his pocket, then held up his frozen dinner. “Guess I won’t need this.”

“Good lord no, that stuff’ll kill you.” Fernando pulled the freezer door open, and a rush of chilled air blew past them. David shivered, but he wasn’t sure if the shudder came because of the cool air or the idea of spending more time with his new friend. He put the dinner back on the shelf.

“You live on Toyon? I have a condo overlooking the country club and golf course… we’re neighbors.” Fernando reached out his hand. “Shall we?”

David nodded and took Fernando’s offered hand. “Okay.” As they moved, “Christmas Wrapping” by The Waitresses started to play over the speaker system. A smile pulled at his lips—“Christmas Wrapping” happened to be one of his favorite songs for this time of year. Muzak’s pick was spot on and reminded him that maybe things happened for a reason and perhaps the universe had a plan all along. “But only if you have real whipped cream for that pie.”

Fernando grinned and pulled him closer. “I have everything, including real whipped cream,” he teased with a wink. “By the way, if you want, we can go for a hike after lunch over at Alum Rock park. I don’t like to just sit around after a big meal.” He patted his flat stomach. “The park’ll be busy with lots of families, hikers, and bikers out and about, so we’ll be perfectly safe, but if you don’t want to go to the park, I’m sure we can find something else to do.” He smirked.

“Oh, nice. Actually, I don’t mind, I’ve been meaning to get up there, but I…” He shook his head. None of that mattered any longer.

After they bought the pie, the frozen dinner and salad left at the store, they walked together, laughing and chatting. Somehow, perhaps thanks in part to meeting Fernando, the day seemed brighter. The assaulting scents of exhaust and petrol that David rushed through earlier seemed to vanish, replaced by aromas of cedar and cinnamon.

"I can't believe we live next to each other, and today is the first we've met." A smile pulled at David's lips.

"You know what I can't believe?" Fernando asked.

David glanced over at him.

"I still don't know your name."

David's eyes grew large and he chuckled. "Oh man, sorry about that. I'm David."

Fernando nodded. "Good to meet you, David." He offered a cheery smile, glancing David up and down again.

David's gaze dropped as he pondered his jeans and purple polo shirt. At least he made an effort in his clothing choices today, not wanting to come to the store in his haunted mansion pajama bottoms and grey t-shirt. Dressing at least somewhat presentable for going out in public was a habit he picked up from his mother, like ensuring he wore fresh underwear every day. Because you never know what's going to happen, she told him and his sister.

Thank goodness.

David bit back a smile at the thought as they continued to walk.

"Typically, I work the holidays and a lot of night shifts," Fernando commented as they continued out of the parking lot.

"What?"

"I was explaining why we haven't run into each other before."

"Ah, right."

"Anyway, I got lucky today and tomorrow, so I'll have a full three days off."

"Three? Why not four?" David asked as he watched a jeep, the car from earlier, back out. In it was the blond guy with a goatee and a brown-haired guy, seemingly sharing a joke and laughing.

"I have a shift Sunday night," Fernando chuckled as he turned from the jeep with the blond driver. He had noticed where David had been looking. "No rest for the wicked, I guess." He focused back on David. "Do you know them?"

David shook his head.

Fernando nodded. "There are a lot of us who live in the area." He smiled, shifting his reusable bag with the pie from one hand to the other. "What about you?"

"I'm off till Monday."

"Excellent," Fernando nodded in the direction they needed to go.

They continued to make their way down the tree-lined street, the walk only a short distance, and David found they were right across the street from his apartment complex. The condo development wasn't large and definitely older than David had originally thought, but as promised, there was a view of the San Jose Golf and Country Club. They made their way up the concrete stairs to the second-floor landing where two doors on opposite walls welcomed them. Fernando handed David the fabric bag with the pie as he fished out his keys and unlocked the front door.

"The condo's not much..." He shrugged and swung open the door. "But it's home."

"At least you own something." David countered. "That's saying a lot. You don't realize how expensive things are until you live here. Even my one-bedroom apartment is insanely overpriced. Right now, I can only dream about buying something, but I keep saving, so who knows."

The two entered the second-floor condo. On David's left a wall covered in a navy raglan geometric wallpaper with a large print picture in a black shiny frame reflecting the modern overhead light. The space underneath the framed picture housed a bench with some shoes located beneath. To the right was a coat closet that Fernando opened to hang his jacket. Along the wall, an opening led to a well-appointed kitchen filled with the smells of roasted turkey, sage, and rosemary. At the end of the hall, painted in a complimentary color to the wallpaper, were a series of black and white photos. You could move either left to what David assumed were the bedrooms and bathrooms, or to the right where you entered a comfortable living room and dining space, both with sliding doors leading to what David assumed to be a balcony. The condo didn't appear huge, but had everything that anyone could need, and the space was a lot bigger than his one-bedroom apartment.

And this place is a lot better decorated.

"Have a seat." Fernando pointed in the direction of the living room. "Can I get you something to drink? Wine, soda, beer, water..."

"I'll have whatever you're having." David walked towards the living room, taking in the space. "I like your walls; the colors really work. You did a great job with this place. I'm jealous."

Fernando laughed. "I had a friend of mine help me decorate a while ago. They finally got tired of my beige walls and crappy furniture. They have a really good eye for this stuff and I'm happy with the results. I had one rule: everything has to be comfortable. There is no way I could live every day with furniture, or whatever, that wasn't relaxing. You know what I mean?"

There was a pop from the kitchen, then what sounded like two glasses being placed on the counter.

"If the decorating were up to me, this place would have continued to look like a frat house with secondhand furniture and beat up floors." He laughed and returned from the kitchen. "White wine okay?"

David nodded. "Perfect. Well, I love the hardwood floors; it really warms up the space and the wood is easy to clean."

Fernando handed David the offered glass of wine before taking a seat in a leather side chair. "Agreed. There is tile in the bathrooms but it's wood everywhere else. I also had to have my big screen TV for my video games." He laughed. "I know I'm a dork."

"Nothing wrong with video games." David took a sip of the wine. "Oh, this is nice."

"Cheers." Fernando leaned back in his chair, taking another sip of the wine.

"Were you really following me around the grocery story?" David asked between sips of wine before placing the wineglass on a coaster he nabbed from the holder. He didn't want to mess up the wood coffee table.

"I would like to lie and say 'no,' but I was." He laughed, before taking another sip. "But I didn't expect you to back into me before I could say hello."

"Well, I can honestly say I've never been picked up in a grocery store." He leaned closer to Fernando, focusing on him.

"Someone as handsome as you? I find that hard to believe," Fernando teased, then placed his glass on his own coaster before standing up.

"Thank you. Given all that has happened, I don't feel handsome these days." Warmth again filled David's cheeks. "Did you need some help in the kitchen? I really hope I'm not putting you out. I can't claim to be a wonderful cook, but I'm happy to be put to work." He stood.

"You're not putting me out." Fernando walked and talked as they moved to the kitchen. "I don't get to enjoy a lot of the holidays off, so when I do get the time, I like to go all out, even if I'm alone. I may not be able to decorate, but cooking is something I'm quite adept at."

David made his way to the kitchen's undermounted porcelain farmhouse sink to wash his hands. "I can smell." He nodded and inhaled all the wonderful aromas. The smells sent him right back home with his parents and sister. "What can I help with?" He put the kitchen towel back on the granite counter where he found it.

"Everything is finished; I was keeping the food warm while I ran to the store. The turkey is the smallest turkey breast I could find, but I'm going to be eating turkey for days, if not weeks." Fernando pulled on some oven mitts and he opened the lower oven. "I left everything in the ovens. I still can't believe I forgot pie." He laughed. "Glad I did, considering how things worked out."

"Me too." David watched as a smallish bowl of mashed potatoes appeared, along with roasted Brussel sprouts, rolls, and what smelled like sage stuffing. "You made all this, just for yourself... why?"

"Well, like I said, I don't get a lot of the holidays off, so why not? My family lives down in Bakersfield, so to get down there for the day is a waste of time unless I'm staying for a couple of days." Fernando checked on the turkey. "And if I'm honest, we don't always get along, so I didn't want the drama."

"Oh, wow, I'm sorry." David offered.

"Don't be." Fernando waved off his comment. "We don't fight about anything major, but someone inevitably has too much to drink and then things get a little out of hand. Plus, you know how the holidays make people." He laughed. "In my family it's not really a holiday until someone ends up slamming a door in tears."

"I guess." David wasn't quite sure how to take that. "My family and I don't usually have those problems, but then I'm the only one who drinks, and never around them."

"Mormon?" Fernando asked.

"Bingo." David responded, placing a finger on the tip of his nose. "Wait, what made you guess that?"

"You said your family was in Utah when we met and with the drinking, I took a guess."

"Ah."

Fernando pulled out the turkey and placed the bird on the gas cooktop as David continued to watch him move around the kitchen, pulling out napkins and utensils. "There is nothing I can help you with?"

"Later," Fernando winked. "You can help with the dishes and clean up."

"Deal."

"Well, the meal is nothing fancy, but everything should be good." Fernando commented, placing the plates he pulled down from the open shelving on the counter.

With everything ready, the two men continued to chit-chat as they loaded up their plates with food and made their way to the dining table that was covered in a golden damask tablecloth. David was not surprised that everything Fernando cooked was as good as it all smelled. The two wouldn't be able to finish everything, no way, but he didn't mind taking a second helping when offered. Even though the day had started off lousy, he really couldn't imagine being anywhere else, besides sitting here with Fernando and enjoying this wonderful meal.

After the afternoon meal, they cleaned up. Instead of having dessert right away, they decided to head up to the park for their walk, which David was grateful for because he didn't want to fall into a food coma after such a delicious meal. And going on a hike would provide more room for what had been promised to be an amazing pie.

We'll see about that. Even if it's not, Fernando has more then made up for it already.

Alum Rock park, as promised, was bustling with families and hikers. The creeks ran high in the later November afternoon, leaving the air cool and crisp. The day really was amazing and spending this time getting to know not only Fernando, but also the park he had been meaning to visit since he moved here, had been perfect. He glanced up and the grey sky had cleared into a bright day with the scents of autumn in the air. A spark of hope and happiness pulled in David's chest. He would have a lot to chat about with his sister later, especially how he had a lot to be thankful for this holiday.

All thanks to a bakery pie and bad timing.

Selected Poetry

Kelliane Parker

HOLIDAY VOYEUR

Holidays past
Wallflower out-skirted
Exiled kin
Tradition resister
Births new observance

Sidewalk voyeur
Holiday windowed
Hallmarked celebrations
Of thresholds
Crossed no more

Now, my heart snow globes
At the thought of her
Match stricken candles
Making shared rituals
Of moon and sun

On her street
I footfall closer
Glacial meltwater
Her name glitters
I snow globe again

Ode to Chosen Family

To the family you have carefully collected
Who come over when the house is a wreck
And quietly make room for take out
From your favorite place
With your favorite dish
Because they know, you know
Who bring orange juice when you're sick
Endure the tedious story about your ex
That they have memorized
But let the recording play
Whose words don't sting
When they say you look crappy
While brushing your hair
Who loved you before you loved your self
Who know the first aid of chocolate and a hug
Whenever they are here
You look around the table
And call it a holiday

Home for the Holidays

Look through the windows of other people's houses
Window's to
Door to heart to possibilities
Of coffee in bed
Hallmarked
I look into her eyes and found home
Outskirts wall flower
Othered
Missed invitation
Gets you off the family guest list
So many missed holidays
And birthdays alone
Window shopping
Walk alone a night and the tv screen

Challah If You Queer Me

Allison Fradkin

When you're a teenager–or, more maturely, a young adult–you are completely at the Mertzy of the *meshugenahs* that are your *mishpocheh.* Yeah, I know–I've got some 'splainin' to do. On the sunny side, I've got minimal complainin' to do. At least in regards to my coming out, which happened the gay–uh, day–of the first night of my sixteenth Hanukkah.

So, picture a nostalgic nuclear family, not unlike the kind you'd find on a black-and-white boob tube. "Which episode should we enjoy this evening?" Dad queries, perusing a pile of VHS tapes. "'Job Switching'? 'Lucy Does a TV Commercial'? 'Lucy and Ethel Buy the Same Dress'?"

"How about 'Gaycation from Marriage'?" I suggest, my stomach twisting like a shofar.

Mom schmears cream cheese on a Tam Tam, as if daring me to make like a matzo and crack. "Is that the one," she asks, noshing on the hexagon, "where the gals are quarreling with the guys and Lucy asks Ethel if she wishes there were something else to marry besides men and Ethel answers 'F yes!' or something a little more fifties-friendly?"

"No, that's the one where Lucy and Ethel take a hiatus from their husbands and move in with each other," Dad mansplains in his customary chivalrous manner. "Then one night, they get all gussied up and pay a visit to their spouses, and Lucy says she hopes Ricky and Fred have as gay an evening as she and Ethel are planning on having and then... Wait."

As Dad's synopsis stops, his eyes grow wider than yarmulkes. The size of Mom's eyes matches macaroons. There's an explosion of silence, unheard of in a Jewish household. Suddenly, I feel like the filling in a blueberry blintz: ready to come out at the slightest provocation. "Mom, Dad," I address my absurdly attentive audience, "I have some seriously super news to share: I'm gay."

Now I hope and wait–and worry that I've just committed a Sapph-faux pas. How will my family react to my declaration of lesbi-independence? Will they regard me like schmutz on a schmatte? Kiss my keppie like everything's kosher? Or offer some verkakte-mamie advice like: "Don't be daffy, Allie. At least date a non-goy boy before you make it official"?

While Mom and Dad–or, more formally, Judy and Steve–turn their wheels like Tevye's milk cart, I start schvitzing like an ice cold bottle of Dr. Brown's cream soda. Maybe they'll do a bottle dance in honor of the unexpected uncapping of my secret?

And then... Judy winks at Steve, and it becomes queer–uh, clear–that the *abba* who knows best has been looking to the *ima* who knows better for approval. I should've known Mom knows.

In our house, we don't practice Judaism. We practice Judyism.

"Better late than straight," the aforementioned mensch guffaws.

"Take me to the WC–the water closet being the only acceptable kind–and call me relieved!" Dad cavorts, his dance a maniacal mishmash of the Horah and the Hokey Pokey.

"Now we don't have to worry about you knocking boots and getting knocked up," Mom marvels, twirling with equivalent merriment.

"And I don't have to compete with another fellow for your attention," Dad discovers. "I have the privilege of being the only man in my little girl's life."

I must be hearing things–which is good, I guess, since I'm hard-of-hearing–but my parents don't really think that my similarities to Sappho are boffo, do they? I mean, it's not like I anticipated yelling, but I definitely did not foresee this degree of glee and kvelling.

"The point is, Allie," Judy says, and I brace myself, because the woman makes more points than a Star of David, "we have *bupkis* to worry about."

Dad's face contorts as if he's just imbibed his first spoonful of Vitameatavegamin. "Nothing at all?" he kvetches.

"Don't worry–we'll think of something," Mom pledges, and Dad perks up pronto.

But then, much to my chagrin–though thank heaven for hearing impairment–they begin to sing a vibrant, validating, verbose version of the *I Love Lucy* theme song:

I love lezzie and she loves me
Queer as happy as two can be
And *chaim* is heaven, you see

'Cause I love lezzie
Yes, I love lezzie
And lezzie loves me!

"Oh, honey," Mom coos, until something shoos the smile off her face. "Stand up straight, my little mezuzah," she demands. "We do expect your posture to be straight." I sigh but comply, her cue to reply with a harrumph of triumph. "Oh, honey, you're home."

As my parents embrace me, squashing me like the childhood of a girl at her Bat Mitzvah, I realize that the bloom isn't off *all* the heteros. In fact, just because one's family *is* nuclear, doesn't mean they'll *go* nuclear at the news that there's a lavender menace in their midst.

"You know," Dad muses, "we should have our own family-friendly TV show: *The Lucy-Lezzie Comedy Hour.*"

"I can see the episodes now!" Mom enthuses. "'Wonder of Wonder, Queer-acle of Queer-acles,' 'Lucy and Ethel Put the Lez in Klezmer,' and the Hanukkah special to end all Hanukkah specials... 'The Labia Menorah'!"

And with that, I am out.

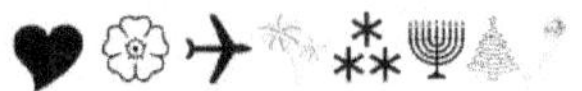

Krampusnacht

Wayne Goodman

Once again, 5 December returns with its chilly night of nasty delight. If children have been disrespectful or ill-behaved, they may be carted off by a nasty, foul-smelling, and goat-like beast with long, tortuous horns. He sweeps the naughty young ones up and tosses them into a big bag slung over his shoulder. A long, sharp tongue lashes out, administering harsh punishment to those youths who deserve it.

And that's me, Krampus. Despite the horrific sounding appearance, I believe I'm rather attractive. However, I've never met another similar being, so that makes comparisons somewhat difficult.

If you've been a bad, bad kid, your only hope of escaping my black sack is to have your parents set out some tasty schnapps for me to drink. I still might sting them with my birch rod if I don't care for the flavor, or I might even strike *you*!

Those do-goodie, nicey-nice children might get some trifling oranges, nuts, or chocolates from that sickeningly jolly Nicholas fellow, but I only dispense punishment and pain for the rest of the lot. I look forward to meeting dreadfully behaved ones with my long-toothed grin, hoping to scare the bejeebers out of you. My sack has plenty of room, so fall right in!

I must admit, it has been lonely all these years, collecting mischievous and wayward children. Saint Nick catches most of the attention. All I get is fruity liquor and the occasional sardonic greeting card. Perhaps if I gave children rewards for their misbehavior they might like me more, but it's just not in my character to provide joyful gifts. Nor would it be appropriate cosmic justice. Penance must be paid. What is a single holiday monster to do?

Marching along the cobbled high street of this nauseatingly charm-filled village in search of little malicious ones keeps me entertained for a while. Candles aflicker in windows and curls of smoke rising from chimneys reveal where potential prey might dwell.

But wait! Who is that exquisite creature at the other end of this gaslit lane? I've never seen anyone like *him* before. Lovely smooth, coal-colored skin and luscious red lips. His feathery outfit looks like he just stepped out of an absurd Shakespearean comedy. And he's carrying a sack as well. I wonder how many children *he* has collected so far.

Oh, no! He draws near. What shall I do? I stand frozen from indecision.

"Hello, I'm Peter!" he warbles in a tuneful tenor. In his outstretched hand, he holds cookies and sweets. "Are you hungry? I think you would enjoy something scrumptious."

What an insult. I require nothing scrumptious, even though *he* looks good enough to eat. My nerves jangle and my mouth waters. Never has this magnificent body responded to someone in such a manner. I remain immobile.

"If you are but a mere statue, I meant you no harm or offence." His broad smile reveals two rows of gleaming teeth. Several dimples deepen into his face.

"I am not a statue!" I roar. My voice echoes from the buildings around us. "I am Krampus, collector of troublesome and unruly children. Do you want to hop into my sack?" I hold the bag open before me.

He peers in. "Oh, my goodness!" He lays his free hand up to the side of that adorable face. "All those boys and girls in there. What did they do to deserve this?"

"They were disrespectful and disobedient. These are bad, bad children."

Peter's brows knit, and he looks up at me with teary eyes. "Children cannot be bad. They are only children. They know not the ways of the world."

"These little ones will get what they deserve!" I peer into the sack. Ruddy, frightened faces with wide, terrified eyes stare back. My heart skips a beat. Such joy. I fling the sack over my bony shoulder.

"Mr. Krampus," the impish Peter coos. "Perhaps I can provide you some company on this long, lonely night." His eyelashes bounce as he blinks a few times.

How could he know of my loneliness? I have only told you, the reader, of my inner thoughts. What magic does this troubling angel possess?

"You cannot lure me with your temptations, Mr. Peter. My only desire is to collect the insubordinate and impertinent. Be on your merry way, spirit!"

His smile broadens, bulging those enchanting, dark cheeks. "You cannot fool me, sir. I feel your desires, and I just want to make you happy."

"*Happy?*" I thunder. "I have *never* been happy, and I hope I never will. Now, be gone with you, alluring sprite."

Peter tilts his head. "Your words reveal inner longings, Mr. Krampus." His eyebrows elevate. "You may have cravings yet to be consummated."

I stomp my foot thrice, shaking snow from surrounding rooftops. "Leave me before I fall ill to your fascinating charms!"

The sack on my back wriggles and writhes. Faint pleas escape the nearly closed opening.

"If you let those children out," Peter chimes, "I can give them all treats. They will be so delighted and very appreciative."

A bellowing laugh erupts from my amused gullet. Echoes travel throughout the lane. "You do intrigue me, my friend."

He gasps. "Are you saying I'm your friend?"

"Not so fast, pucky boy." I hold up an open palm. "We are not friends, nor will we ever be, no matter how eye-fetching you are. And another thing." I point the free hand over my shoulder. "These bad, bad children will never, *ever* be set free. I will eat them later. Their fates are sealed!"

"Well… it appears there is nothing I can do to change your mind, so, I will take my leave. I wish you all the best, Mr. Krampus." He turns and strides away.

"Wait! Where are you going?"

He stops and faces me. "I have many more children to visit tonight, as do you. Let us tarry no longer than necessary. Hail and farewell." Off he trots.

"But what about…?"

His gloved hand waves above the plume-laden velvet cap.

"What time will you be finished?" I yell after him.

Peter scurries back to me. "About the same as you, I imagine. Why?"

My head drops. "No reason. Go away."

"I think you would like to know more about me. Am I correct, Mr. Krampus?"

My body shudders. "Mr. Krampus was my father. Call me Kelson."

"All right… Kelson. Perhaps we might meet up once our work is complete."

I shrug my shoulders, eliciting cries of terror from the lost souls in my black bag.

"If we sit by a warm, toasty fire, I could tell you a story." Peter beams and leans forward. "Have you ever heard 'Androcles and the Lion'…?"

View From the Bridge

Alexandra Caluen

Chapter 1

Wednesday, December 18, 2019
Jimmy

Since my return to San Francisco, I had yet to enter a restaurant that wasn't incredibly busy and incredibly loud. Fortunately, "loud" is my middle name, so I yelled across the bar to my manager, "Linda, hi! Sorry I'm late!" She spotted me, nodded, and said something to the host. The other paralegals in my group had all turned when they heard my dulcet tones, making various faces that mostly added up to amusement. I'd only been with the group for six months, but this wasn't our first gathering. Between colliding at the coffee machine in the break room, discussing cases in somebody's office over lunch, getting down to street level at some point in the afternoon for a snack break, and heading out for drinks together, I hadn't had a chance to miss any of my old Navy cohort or more-recent work colleagues back in San Diego.

Well, okay, I missed the ones I hooked up with, and presumably they missed me. Most of them were like, "Oh, damn, you lucky bastard," when they heard I was coming home. Then I told them exactly *why* I was coming home and they were like, "Oh, shit, you poor bastard." But I could put all that aside tonight, because we were heading in for our pre-holiday group dinner and I was feeling festive. Also hungry, and the place smelled amazing.

Then I caught someone's eye across the bar and stopped in my tracks. We just stared at each other for a moment. You know how it is when you see someone who ticks a lot of your boxes, and then they're looking at you as if you might tick a lot of *their* boxes, and then one of you kind of smiles? Yeah, that. He smiled back. I swear, if I hadn't been there with people, I would have plowed right across the bar. But somebody took my arm and said, "Come *on*, Jimmy," and I let myself be dragged into the main dining room.

Ren

His name was Jimmy. Somehow, I caught that. You would think, after a lot of years risking my hearing in noisy environments up to and including flight decks, I might've missed it. Apparently, he was at the restaurant for the same reason as me: a work gathering. I'd heard those were a real Thing among the corporate offices here in San Francisco; judging from the half-dozen groups gradually forming in the bar, the rumor was accurate. I was early, as usual, so when the cute guy–Filipino, I thought–vanished into the other room I turned back to the bar and my drink. Once my group finally assembled, we were seated on the far side of the dining room. We made our own fair share of noise, but Jimmy's table kept catching my attention. When I saw him stand up (obviously not to leave for the night, so he might be headed for the restroom) I also got to my feet. Excused myself and made my way to the hallway. Sure enough, there he was, waiting outside two closed doors.

"You'd think they'd have more than a pair of singles in a place like this," he remarked as I stopped beside him, glancing up at me in a friendly way.

"You would think that," I agreed, as if we'd been in the middle of a conversation and already knew each other. Because we weren't and didn't, I dug out a business card. "Hi. Looks like you and your group are having a good time."

He took the card, glanced at it, and raised his gaze to mine with a smile. "Hello, Ren Itano. My name's Jimmy."

"Yes, I heard."

He laughed. "I didn't think of bringing my cards. I do have my phone, though." Without further ado, he pulled it out of his pocket, entered my mobile number, and sent me a text. I felt the vibration as it landed. Then the restroom door opened and a soused-looking white man shuffled out. I lifted a hand to indicate Jimmy should go in next. He gave me another glance–and I don't mind saying it was flirty–before the door closed behind him. A moment later, the other door opened, and a young woman exited. I went in to take care of business, which included checking the text.

It read: *Jimmy Rubio here. Busy after dinner?*

I texted back: *No, want to get a drink?*

By the time I returned to my group, a reply had landed. I couldn't resist looking at it. Smiled when I did. *Catch up with you outside.*

Jimmy

It was fucking cold when we all finally staggered out of the restaurant. I dug into my messenger bag for the knitted chenille rainbow scarf one of my co-workers gave me, wrapped it around my neck as many times as it would go, and finished the look with a purple corduroy newsboy cap. Only when I was protected from the elements did I look around for the Japanese American silver fox of a lawyer. He was standing about twelve feet from the parking valet, wearing a Navy pea coat and a slight smile. I toddled over there and said, "Next door?" Because of course there was an establishment next door, drinking, for the purpose of.

"I'd invite you over to my place, but it's across the bridge."

And I wasn't going over any bridges tonight, but "my place" sounded better than a bar, and while my place wasn't the Ritz, it was private. Ren's expression confirmed my inclination toward privacy. "Well, I live in Outer Richmond."

"Do you need to get your car?"

"No, I take the bus to Market Street and caught an Uber here." We eyed each other. "There's an off-street parking space."

Ren smiled. "How about I give you a lift home?"

Chapter 2

That night
Ren

I followed Jimmy's prompts, provided in a way that told me he was an experienced navigator, to the slightly shabby residential neighborhood between Geary Boulevard and Golden Gate Park. The row house he directed me to was second from a corner, with the typical downward-sloping driveway beside stairs up to an entrance portico secured by wrought-iron grillwork. I said, "Okay if I back in?"

"Sure." He waited until I'd set the parking brake, the bumper within a few inches of the garage door, before saying, "Two things you should know. I live with my mother, she stays upstairs, and I have a cat. Wait, that's three things."

I stifled a laugh. "All three of those things are fine. You're living in the garage?"

"It's temporary," he said as we got out of the car. "I've been back here for six months and it's taking forever to get the place livable. My dad was a hoarder." He unlocked the trade door on the far side of the front steps and beckoned me in. "And my brother was just as bad. He died in a car accident last May."

"Oh, my goodness. I'm so sorry."

Jimmy flipped a light switch and locked the door behind us. "Thanks, me too. We didn't really get along, but he was my only sibling. Luckily the firm I worked for in SD has an office here and let me transfer." Then, with an air of "let's talk about something else," he pointed past me. "Behold, my bachelor pad."

I followed him into the basement. A car, presumably his, was parked on the ramp. A sturdy bicycle leaned against a mountain of storage bins and boxes. The bulk of the space was partitioned off from the ramp by a back-to-back double row of cabinets and bookcases. The side walls of the garage were roughly finished: studded out, insulated, mostly clad with OSB and covered with what I found to be old Automobile Club maps. "These make terrific wallpaper," I said. "From the hoard?"

"You got it. Forty Niner, meet Ren Itano. Ren, this is my feline bed-warmer."

I approached the unexpectedly beautiful bed, which stood on a large piece of nondescript carpet layered with Oriental-style area rugs. Chinese rosewood, covered with multiple quilts, topped with a fake-fur throw. Maybe he simply liked the layered style, but the effect was warm and inviting. A huge Himalayan cat sprawled in the center of the throw. "Forty Niner. Football or history?"

"History," Jimmy said, looking pleased. "We have a Chinese ancestor who came over during the Gold Rush." He watched as I offered a cautious hand to the cat, was duly sniffed, and turned back to the man. Then he indicated the utility wall. "So, there's my little kitchen. You want an actual drink? Or I could make tea."

"Tea would be nice," I said.

Jimmy

Unfazed by the basement or the cat, Ren pleased me further by choosing tea. I would've poured us some whatever, but a nonalcoholic beverage meant we were likely to talk a bit more before booting Niner off the bed. I filled my electric kettle at the utility sink and switched it on, indicating the wall-mounted shelf that was my pantry and dishrack. "Choose your preference? I need to run upstairs and check on Mom."

"Okay."

I gave him a smile and headed for the stairs. The next few minutes would be ample time for Ren to make some observations. My personal items were mixed into a curated selection of Dad's things on the bookshelves. The hoarding gene passed me by, which facilitated living in base housing or studio apartments for most of my career; my San Diego residence had packed up into a small U-Haul trailer. But I did have things that spoke to who I was, like framed pictures from my Navy years, a framed college diploma, and souvenirs from my travels. I'd been all over the world in the past thirty years. Which was a good thing, because I probably wouldn't be going much of anywhere as long as Mom was alive.

She was fine, as usual, if slightly confused, also as usual. I made sure she'd had something to eat; refilled the water bottle on her bedside table; told her a short funny story from the evening's dinner; and said, "I've got company but don't be afraid to ring the intercom if you need anything."

"Oh Jimmy, did you bring home a boy?"

"I brought home a lawyer," I said, in a way that said she should be impressed. She laughed, which was also an acceptable response. "He's very nice and I didn't poach him from my own firm. I'll see you in the morning, okay?"

"Okay."

I kissed her goodnight and headed back downstairs via the bathroom (to make sure it was in good shape for the next day) and the kitchen (likewise). Mom had non-Alzheimer's dementia, mild enough that she could mostly take care of herself; still, attention must be paid. There were days I found her hearing aid in the refrigerator or the newspaper in the laundry basket. But I wasn't thinking about that tonight, because when I got downstairs, I found a handsome man sitting in one of the two rosewood corner chairs flanking the electric fireplace. All three items were unearthed from the hoard, like my grandmother's bed. Ren was calmly reading Hafiz (also unearthed from the hoard), affecting not to mind the cave-like atmosphere. At least it was a clean, tidy cave now, after four consecutive weekends of family picking-over, donation deliveries, and 1-800-Got-Junk collection. More remained to be done, but it was a tolerable interim bedroom. Especially with this man sitting in it. "Did I have a tea you like?"

He looked up at me and smiled. "I should have asked what *you'd* like. The tea could be ready by now."

"I'm not in a hurry," I said, returning his smile.

Chapter 3

Thursday
Ren

Jimmy must have had the fireplace on a timer; his basement bedroom was comfortably warm when my phone alarm went off. "Mmph," he said, screwing up his face in a way that said he was not yet ready to wake.

"Sorry," I said, nuzzling his cheek. "I have to get home so I can catch the ferry."

"Too bad we don't wear the same size," he said lazily. Then he blinked, as if he'd heard himself and couldn't believe what he'd said.

I stifled a laugh. "It's a shame," I agreed. "This is an extremely comfortable bed."

"Even with the giant furball?"

"He kept my feet warm." Jimmy was staring at me, body cuddly and relaxed against mine. Well, not entirely relaxed. I needed to get out of bed before I got any more turned on. So why did I lean in and kiss him? Maybe because I spent quite some time doing quite a few things with that sweet mouth last night and couldn't think of a better way to start the day. I kept trying to stop; kept not stopping.

Finally, he pushed me gently away, laughing. "You're gonna be hating life if you don't get out of here pronto."

"Mmm, I know. This was great, Jimmy."

"Yeah. Glad we met."

I didn't really intend to make any suggestions before I left. In the few minutes it took to refresh and dress (the unheated basement half-bath did not invite leisurely ablutions), I told myself not to make the next move. Then he unlocked the trade door for me, and I fell into his mouth again. When we parted, I said, "Ever been to Sausalito?"

He smiled. "Is that an invitation?"

I smiled back. "I'll text you." I meant to send a casual note later, like around lunchtime. Instead, I took a picture of the bridge, barely visible through fog, from the deck of the ferry and sent that. A reply came in just as

I left the elevator at my office: *Looks cold. Do you need a cat on your feet?* Which made me smile again.

My assistant said, "Good morning, Mr. Itano," as I passed.

"Good morning," I said. "Anything hot?"

"Nope. The world seems to know it's only got a few functional business hours before Christmas."

"Great. Cross your fingers."

"You bet!"

I'd get her a coffee later, the way I usually did. Too bad I couldn't tell her about the cute Legalman I picked up last night. What were the odds two ex-Navy men would run into each other at unrelated work gatherings? That we'd be within a couple years of the same age, that we'd both now be working in civilian law, that we'd both only recently settled in San Francisco, that we'd instantly connect?

Making the transition from the JAG Corps to of-counsel in an international firm had been less difficult than expected, but it hadn't left much time to meet people. I'd barely even begun thinking I should *try* to meet people. On the few occasions when hunger and loneliness got the best of me, an app led me to relief. Thank all the gods I still photographed decently. And that, apparently, quite a few young men were actively looking for a "daddy." I wasn't going to be that guy, but I wasn't above meeting someone for a no-strings hookup.

Which was really all I'd expected from Jimmy. But last night was wonderful, and today we somehow exchanged a long string of texts. His last one read: *So what's the main attraction in Sausalito.*

Jimmy

Okay, that was a sassy little text, but, honestly, we'd been going back and forth all day. Which was *not* what I would've expected, if I'd had any expectations at all. A pleasant cup of tea followed by some very attentive oral sex followed by unusually restful co-sleeping followed by a mind-blowing kiss at the door; not what I expected! I thought we'd go home, toss back a slug of bourbon, and get each other off in the most expedient fashion. I thought he would then zip himself up and drive off into the night. I did not think we'd wake up smiling, ready to go again, prevented only by the exigencies of working life.

Fuck work, anyway. Or rather: dammit, work, I was primed for a fuck.

In any case, waking up like that put me in an extremely good mood. Getting an artful picture of the Golden Gate Bridge before I was even dressed did nothing to bring me down. Then the fact that he seemed to enjoy my teasing? Best day I'd had since I moved back to town, if I'm honest.

And the hits just kept on coming. Ren's reply to my sass was: *Meet me on the outer bikepath, middle of GG, Saturday between 0815 and 0830, and find out.*

To which I replied: *You'd better make it worth my while.*

To which he replied: *Guaranteed.*

To which I replied nothing, because I was giggling to myself, trying to uncurl my toes, generally high on life. Even though I'd just committed to biking eight miles and change, which I hadn't yet done here in SF, and it was bound to be cold as hell.

I'd be warm by the time we got to Sausalito. Especially if this meeting was some kind of seriousness and/or compatibility test proceeding directly to Ren's condo, breakfast, and that fuck I mentioned.

Chapter 4

That Night

Jimmy

Thursday night at home was the usual: watching something on TV with Mom while we ate dinner and discussed (again) the relative merits of inviting anybody over for Christmas. I wasn't inclined to. We'd already turned down invitations from a couple of my aunties to join their gatherings. I love my extended family, don't get me wrong. But a holiday at somebody's house was always the *entire* day, with anywhere from a dozen to two dozen people involved, and we'd feel obligated to bring gifts as well as something to eat. When it comes right down to it, I didn't care to use that much of my precious free time to (A) shop or (B) assemble a dish to share, and Mom was past that now. Anyway, I was looking forward to an extra day off. You could have knocked me over with a feather when Mom said, "Do you want to invite your friend?"

There was no doubt in my mind she meant Ren. I blinked. Stared at her. Tried to think of something to say that wasn't "you know that was a hookup, right." In the end I said, "Uh, now that you mention it, we kind of have a date Saturday."

"Good, you can ask him then."

What?!

She must have seen that on my face. Sometimes Mom was still very sharp. She said, "Were you planning to stay the night with him? Because your cousin Lee said she could come."

My mouth must have been hanging open; I had to close it to swallow. Cleared my throat and said, "Uh, let me text her." Which I immediately did. Not because I *expected* to spend the night at Ren's place, but because it would be awfully nice to have the option. Lee replied in a few minutes, saying she'd be happy to Mom-sit on Saturday night. #AwesomeCuz.

Friday
Jimmy

Along with work, I had two non-work things to do: hint to Ren that I was available for at least twenty-four hours from our rendezvous on Saturday, and shop for a present for Lee. Because sure, she was family, and she offered, but I knew how it felt to be taken for granted. She was doing me a favor; ergo, I should show my appreciation. Thus, my lunch hour found me over at the Ferry Building marketplace. I was sitting with a coffee and a sandwich, gloating over the assembled gift basket, when someone sat down across from me. "That all looks delicious."

I glanced up and couldn't stop the smile. "Ren!"

"I was going to text you when I got back to the office."

"This is better," I said. "You look great."

"Likewise."

I did a coy little half-shrug thing. I'm basically a Kewpie doll: short, somewhat rounded, and mostly bald. Thanks, DNA. Regardless, I have a long history of being considered cute and getting plenty of action because of it. Ren's expression told me I could get as much as I wanted from him. I said, "If I had hair like yours, I'd grow it down to my butt." Because his was thick, wavy, and steel gray. Yum.

Ren laughed. Sipped from his own coffee cup, eyeing me. "We still on for tomorrow?"

"Yes, we are. In fact, this," I indicated the basket, "is for my cousin Lee, who volunteered to Mom-sit Saturday night." Judging from Mr. Ex JAG's expression, that was good news.

Friday
Ren

I sipped again, mentally trying out a few versions of the next thing to say. In the end, I went with, "I was going to ask how much time you might have to spare." Jimmy, mouth full of sandwich, made a grand "now you know" gesture. I leaned closer to the basket, assessing the contents. A generous gift by any measure.

"I got her a spa certificate too," Jimmy said. "Soften her up for the next demand." I laughed again. He nudged my foot with his under the table. "Anything there you'd hate?"

"Hmm. No." Thus we told each other more about ourselves. We'd done a lot of that since Wednesday night. Hard to believe I'd only known him for two days. I glanced at my watch and sighed. "Have to get back to the office."

"Yeah, me too. Text tonight if anything changes?"

I nodded and got to my feet, sketching a wave. His mouth was full of sandwich again, so I didn't lean down to kiss him. I wanted to, though.

Chapter 5

Saturday
Ren

I was leaning against the bridge railing, back to the wind, gazing east toward the city, when Jimmy rolled up beside me. "It's absolutely fucking awful out here," he announced as he stopped his bike.

My feelings: relief, delight, and excitement. It was a gray, cold, intermittently wet morning, and I wouldn't have blamed him for texting some kind of counteroffer. But here he was, doing things the hard way, and it couldn't possibly be for any reason other than he wanted to. Despite the weather, he was bright-eyed and smiling. Irresistible. "It's pretty awful," I agreed. "There's a fireplace in my condo."

"Ooh! A real one?"

How did he always make me laugh? "No, it's gas."

"Fine, whatever. Can we go? Because my inner house cat is spitting mad."

I was grinning as I threw a leg over my bike. Grinning most of the way home, to be honest, despite the wind, drizzle, and traffic. There weren't many other bicyclists on the path, but a lot of people were already out in their cars. The last weekend before Christmas meant shoppers. Since we both needed to pay attention, I didn't try to converse as we rode. Only when I scanned my key card to open the gate at my complex did I say, "How much shopping did you have to do?"

"Almost none," Jimmy said. "Mom and Lee, basically. How about you?"

"I only have people back in Japan now," I said. "Took care of my mother and my sister's family early this month."

"Oh! Nobody here?"

"No." We were walking our bikes toward my unit; I turned my head to make eye contact.

Jimmy met my gaze and, with an air of "here goes nothing," said, "Mom said I should invite you over if you don't already have plans for Christmas Day."

I was speechless for a moment. Then: "I wasn't hinting, but that's very nice."

"So, would you like to? No pressure. Super casual. Just the three of us."

"Four," I said. "Counting Forty Niner." Jimmy grinned. I unlocked the garage door and rolled it up so we could park our bikes inside. Closed the door again to keep the weather out. We unbuckled helmets, wiping them off with the towels I kept handy; shook off our all-weather jackets and hung them from convenient ceiling hooks. Shed our cycling shoes at the kitchen door and padded into the condo.

Once the door was closed behind us and we were in the warm, I turned to Jimmy again. "I wanted to kiss you at the marketplace yesterday."

"Oh." He smiled. "Sandwich got in the way, huh." Tipping his chin up, lips slightly parted, inviting me to dive in. I'd meant to offer a warm drink by the fire, but five minutes later we were naked in bed.

Jimmy

Somewhere around ten o'clock I stretched luxuriously and said, "You did say you'd make it worth my while." Ren laughed into the pillow. I nudged his leg with my toe. "Gee, and it's not even noon. Whatever shall we do for the rest of the day?"

He rolled over, smiling, mouth reddened from our ravenous kisses. Hair mussed, eyes sleepy, expression eloquent of contentment. "If the weather was better, I'd suggest taking the kayak out."

"No," I said firmly. He laughed again. I did not find that in any way offensive. In fact, I was delighted. If people laughed when I meant them to, it was usually a very good sign. And we were sure racking those up. If he continued to be this perfect all the way through Christmas, I'd have to ask if he'd like to be boyfriends. Hadn't had one of those for what seemed like a long time. I stretched again, wriggling my back, savoring the welcome ache in my ass. "Gawd, that felt good." Now he blushed, the faintest wash of pink over his cheeks and nose. I leaned in to kiss him, ever so lightly. "What do you need to know?"

Ren blinked. "About what?"

"About me, or Mom, or the hoard house, or whatever. I have a million questions for you, so it's only fair."

He shifted enough to get a hand on me. Patted gently, then stroked my appreciative skin with his thumb. "I do have questions. How about a cup of tea by the fire?"

"Mmm, yeah. Quick shower first?"

Half an hour later, we were cozily curled on the couch, not too much space between us. He'd offered a choice of teas. For this particularly unlovely winter day, I selected Bohea and let it brew as dark as coffee. Sweetened with local raw honey and softened with milk, it was delicious. I lifted my mug in a mock toast. "So? First question?"

And, oh, my goodness, if I hadn't already been fully infatuated, Ren's next words would've tipped me over the edge. "How in the world are you single?"

"Me?! That's exactly what I was going to ask *you*!"

Chapter 6

Sunday
Ren

By morning we'd run out of questions for each other. Jimmy knew all about my last posting in Japan, which I'd campaigned for so I could be close to my family. My sister, born in the U.S. like me, had married a Japanese citizen and moved there years ago. Our mother joined their household after our father died.

Jimmy's story wasn't too different. Maneuvering for a California posting after his father died, staying in San Diego after separating from the Navy. Moving into civilian employment, because he was too young to retire. Jimmy told me about some of his past boyfriends and lovers; I shared a few stories of my own. We'd joined the service within a year of each other in the late 1980s, lived through "Don't Ask, Don't Tell," and come out within days of its repeal being effected. Jimmy said none of his people were surprised; a few of mine were. "They must not have been paying attention," he said. "A guy as good-looking as you who doesn't have women hanging all over him *has* to be gay."

"I changed post pretty often," I said, amused. "After the initial meet-and-greets, nobody questioned the absence of a wife."

He fiddled with the hem of his sweater. "Speaking of. Did you ever consider getting married?"

"Oh, of course. I had a good friend in the Corps, and we talked about it a few times. She wanted to have kids. That was almost twenty years ago, and for a moment I was tempted. But in the end, I couldn't commit to it. Never wanted to be a parent."

"Me either," Jimmy said. "Maybe because I grew up with relays of kids in the house. Cousins and second cousins and step-siblings of cousins. I've changed more than my fair share of diapers, let me tell you. And I wanted to travel! I mean, you don't join the Navy to grow roots, do you?"

I smiled. Shook my head. Moved a hand closer to him. "I didn't want to live alone forever, though."

He moved his hand, enough that our little fingers overlapped. "I didn't either. I always suspected, you know, I'd end up looking after Mom. Either my brother would flake out on us, or something would happen."

I'd already heard about the drinking, the weed habit, the marginal employment history. Sometimes it's hard to believe two people come from the same genetic material. "So, you thought you'd eventually come back to San Francisco."

Jimmy nodded. "I have so many people here. Even the ones who were appalled to have a gay boy in the family are over it now. They've been like, 'Ooh, here's a picture of my co-worker,' or 'Hey, I met this cute guy at the garden center.'" I laughed. He gave me a sardonic look. "And then there's the queer law network."

"Oh, my goodness, yes." As we both snickered, I became aware of a drumming sound and turned my head to see rain pouring down outside. "Well. Good thing we didn't take the kayak out."

Jimmy

"There was literally no chance of that," I said. "I don't even want to ask you to *drive* in this shit."

"I don't mind. I certainly wouldn't make you ride your bike home."

I wriggled suggestively. "My ass thanks you." He blushed again. You would think this guy never had a flirty little twerp like me around. Well, maybe he didn't; Ren was All Dignity, versus my All Nonsense. Even when he was unraveling in bed, he did it with class. I could very happily have spent a whole 'nother day with him, but Lee would be expecting me home at a decent hour. Like, before noon. Which meant, "I really don't want to leave at all, but I probably should."

"Yes." He said it on a sigh. Before I had a chance to internally question what that meant–was it pure disinclination to leave the house, or was he specifically not ready to get rid of me–he answered the unspoken query. "I like having you here."

We stared at each other. I swallowed. "Maybe I should prioritize getting one of the upstairs bedrooms livable." Almost a question.

Ren said, "You know, the bachelor pad is pure luxury compared to some of my billets."

And now we were both smiling. "Come for Christmas," I said. "And we'll see if there's a place you could hang some clothes."

Chapter 7

Christmas Day
Jimmy

Before she left on Sunday, Lee helped me reorganize the dining room. It was still hoard-like, but at least it was now navigable and clean. I promised I'd have her over for dinner soon, thanked her again, and sent her on her way before she could offer to help upstairs. There was no point making myself crazy about the top-floor situation. I'd told Ren it was a matter of goat trails through mountains of crap, a tour would only make him question the family sanity, and if he wanted a sample that wouldn't embarrass me to tears, he could see the home office behind the kitchen.

In the interest of Being Ready for Company, I drove to work on Monday and Tuesday, grateful I had the choice *not* to run errands via bus. This meant that on Christmas morning, literally all I needed to do was assemble a semi-festive array of foods, choose a bottle or two of wine (thanks, Dad; that part of the hoard was useful!), and run around with the hand vac to catch any stray tumbleweeds of cat hair. Well, and obsess about how consequential this day felt. Ren was due around noon, and I was suddenly very nervous about it.

Mom dressed up in her best bright red velour tracksuit, with a matching Santa hat. I squeezed into a pair of skinny jeans and a Fair Isle-inspired sweater featuring classic Atari icons. I'd just finished tweaking the arrangement of fake pine garland and hurricane lamps on our fireplace mantel when the doorbell rang. I sped to the front door and yanked it open. Ren smiled at me from the far side of the security gate. I was so glad to see him. "Hi! How was traffic?"

"A lot of people were coming into the city today."

I had the gate open; Ren stepped inside, offering a glossy red gift bag. "You didn't have to bring anything."

"Just to say thank you for the invitation." He correctly interpreted my expression and gave me a quick kiss.

A second later, we heard Mom. "Jimmy, bring him inside!"

I rolled my eyes at Ren, we both stifled a laugh, and I closed the door. Peeked into the bag as we walked into the living room. "Ooh! Mom, he brought us some fancy tea!"

"That's nice. Merry Christmas," she said to Ren. "I'm Beverly."

"Ren," he said, taking her offered hand. "So pleased to meet you. Thank you for including me today."

"I'm glad you could come. Jimmy's been working so hard since he came home, I don't know if he's even spoken to his old friends."

"I have," I reminded her. "I'm going to put this in the kitchen. Do we want some tea or coffee? Or there's that sherry I got in Spain, or champagne?"

Mom said, "Ooh! Let's have champagne."

Ren

I had a list–compiled from our ongoing text exchange–of topics to avoid in conversation. Those included Jimmy's father, his brother, and the hoard. "She doesn't really see it," he'd said when we spoke the night before. "If you could pretend it all looks normal, I'd appreciate it."

Aside from the home office, it really wasn't bad. Boxes were stacked behind the loveseat that shared the living room with two recliners and a large cat tree (occupied by Forty Niner). The dining room featured a black lacquer table and chairs for eight. A room-spanning window seat was completely covered with stacks of photo albums, framed pictures, and a variety of vintage trophies. A graceful tea *tansu* stood in a corner, with an arrangement of family pictures on the wall above it. Three generations of Rubio men in uniform, sepia-toned photos of what had to be great-grandparents, a very old postcard from Manila, and a wedding picture. Beverly and her husband, looking impossibly young. I didn't ask any questions.

On the outside wall were three vintage breakfronts, each displaying a full set of china. The Chinoiserie black lacquer one must be Beverly's. The others, Chippendale-style mahogany and midcentury maple, probably came from his two grandmothers. Many family legends had to revolve around those dishes. Maybe someday I'd hear them.

Jimmy said his mother loved travel stories, and I had plenty of those. Between the two of us we kept things lively through the champagne, some savory appetizers, and dinner. Over dessert, we all compared impressions of Hawaii and Guam, the two places outside the continental U.S. that Beverly had visited. "Those tropical gardens were so beautiful," she said, "but nothing like that will grow here. I want to put a Japanese garden in our backyard."

"Do you? What's there now?"

Jimmy made an "eek" face and said, "A lot of weeds. Low priority."

"I love a Japanese garden too," I told Beverly. "Have you been to the one in Golden Gate Park recently?"

For the first time, she seemed uncertain. "I don't think so?"

"Not since I moved home," Jimmy said, looking guilty. "I'll take you soon, Mom. We'll try for a day when it's not so cold."

"Maybe Ren could come with us," she said craftily.

Jimmy's eyes went wide, his expression a clear apology. Why he would apologize, I didn't know. Why the idea of a family outing to the park was so attractive, I knew very well. "I'd love to," I said with perfect honesty. "My Sundays are nearly always free."

"So maybe," Jimmy said a few minutes later, when the two of us were loading the dishwasher, "you could spend a Saturday night here sometime."

"I'd love to," I said again. Got a hand on him and tugged him into my arms, where he fit so perfectly. Bent my head and kissed him.

His mother was in the next room, so I didn't lose myself the way I wanted to. When we separated, Jimmy blinked his starry eyes. Swallowed, took a breath, and said very softly, "Are we boyfriends now?"

I ran my thumb over his succulent lower lip. We were both smiling. I said, "I hope we are."

Home Alone

Andrew Beierle

'Twas the night before Christmas, when all through the house
Not a creature was stirring, not even the louse;
No stockings were hung by the chimney with care,
The larder was empty; the cupboard was bare.

I suppose you could say I learned the true meaning of Christmas in 1965. I was fourteen years old, my mother had been dead for four years, and I had spent the previous two Christmas holidays in foster care–in 1963 with kindly, self-appointed guardians, the parents of one of my seventh-grade classmates; the next year with a court-appointed family of alleged do-gooders headed by a matriarch who would give Cruella de Vil a run for her money. But it took a Christmas with Daddy Dearest, a.k.a. "the louse," to finally transform me into a true and lifelong Ebenezer Scrooge.

In fact, my brother and sister and I did not call the louse "Daddy," dearest or otherwise. By this time, we had concocted for him the name "Father-o," a term of endearment with a sarcastic twist. *Father-o,* like the beatnik term *Daddio* we'd picked up from watching *The Dobie Gillis Show.* "Far out, Daddio." It was our way of distancing ourselves from the unfortunate but irrefutable fact of our blood relationship with this man, this stranger, this sperm donor who occupied our home and our lives as we were growing up.

I was never close to my father. For one thing, he was an alcoholic–an angry drunk, bellowing and bellicose, whose arguments with my mother sent the three of us kids scuttling to our rooms while crockery and epithets flew through the air in our modest tract house in suburban Philadelphia. For another, I suspect he knew there was something different about his second son, the baby of the family, which did little to endear me to him. I was, undeniably, a sissy. I had been a premature baby and had spent time in an incubator at birth, an experience that may have saved my life but which I believe also marked me, in his mind, as somehow weak or defective. I gravitated toward my sister–sometimes to her chagrin–when she was playing with dolls or picking out dress patterns. I lisped. I exclaimed, "Oh, dear!" so often he forbade me to ever utter those words again. At an amusement park, while my brother enjoyed riding roller coasters, I screamed and cried on a merry-go-round, convinced the brightly painted horse was going higher and higher with each revolution and that I was about to fall off, even though my mother was standing next to me with one hand on my shoulder and another on my thigh.

I have no recollection of ever enjoying his company. We never played catch or went camping or fishing together–not that I would have enjoyed *any* of those activities. I do remember, however, spending a *lot* of time with him in taprooms, drinking Shirley Temple cocktails while seated next to him at the bar on red-padded stools, the air smoky and overly chilled, the glass-topped counter somehow both sticky and slippery with condensation. Maybe it was some form of babysitting. I was three years younger than my sister, nearly five years my brother's junior, so it's possible that when my mother was shopping or getting her hair done, he was responsible for me. But it seems more likely I was something of a "beard" for him when driving drunk. We lived just a few miles from the Delaware River, the boundary between Pennsylvania and New Jersey. On Sundays, when Pennsylvania's blue laws shut down taverns, my father would drive across the river to Trenton, where he could drink and buy draft beer in cardboard containers to bring home. I accompanied him on one such trip. On our return, he drove the wrong way onto the Trenton-Morrisville bridge. Oncoming traffic parted around us like the Red Sea before Moses, headlights flashing, tires squealing, shrieking horns providing a vivid demonstration of the Doppler effect. Maybe he thought a patrolman would be less likely to arrest him for DUI if he also had to figure out what to do with a six-year-old kid.

But I digress. The story at hand is the one in which, like McCauley Culkin, I found myself home alone on Christmas Eve.

Until my mother died from complications of childhood rheumatic fever in 1961, we lead a reasonably normal life–and we celebrated Christmas like any other family. We hung our stockings on the mantel, lined our front windows with alternating red and green lights, and decorated our tree with my grandmother's hand-blown ornaments from Eastern Europe in the shape of exotic birds. Throughout the year, we dutifully deposited fifty cents a week into our "Christmas Club" accounts, accruing a mind-boggling $25 in time for holiday shopping. Invariably, I bought my father selections from the Old Spice lineup of men's grooming products. It was a no-brainer, year-to-year, requiring little thought and no emotional investment. Old Spice made it easy by introducing new variations. I was particularly tickled by the "soap-on-a-rope" concept, and we were all delighted when they came out with a fragrance called "Burley," one of the many ways in which our last name could be mispronounced.

But things fell apart after our mom's death–and not only at Christmas. I am guessing she had been a moderating influence on my father. Their most explosive arguments were about his drinking–taking place, of course, when he was drunk. With her out of the picture, his drinking got worse. He lost his job as a foreman at a US Steel mill when he showed up for work drunk. I later learned that the gate guards would have been satisfied to turn him away and have him call in sick, but he became belligerent and forced the issue.

Over the next two years, our once stable and predictable home life deteriorated dramatically. Bills went unpaid. Telephone service and heating oil deliveries were suspended and reinstated with the unpredictability of a roulette wheel. Government surplus cheese, evaporated milk, and dehydrated eggs became staple foodstuffs. At one point, my father was interned in a detox program at the notorious Philadelphia State Hospital known as Byberry.

In the fall of 1963, I pricked a finger while pinning on a campaign button for our seventh-grade class treasurer. I was so malnourished that my finger became grossly infected and came to the attention of family friends who had done their best to monitor our situation after my mother's death. They removed both me and my sister from our home and placed us with two sets of neighbors, who like them also were stationed at the Willow Grove Naval Air Station. My brother, at sixteen, was deemed old enough to fend for himself. When the family who was caring for me was transferred to the Naval Air Station at Alameda, California, in March 1964, they petitioned for custody but were denied. I became a ward of the court for the next year, until my father was deemed responsible enough to care for me again–a point that for me was still open to debate.

I don't recall my sister's whereabouts on Christmas Eve of 1965. She was a senior in high school with a part-time job and was more independent than me. But neither she nor my father were home as the neighborhood Christmas lights twinkled on in late afternoon, and I was fairly certain neither would return until the next day.

At the age of fourteen, I had long given up my belief in Santa Claus, but I was still hopeful enough to want Christmas gifts. It was the whole *point* of the holiday, after all. Even in my two foster homes, I had received presents on Christmas morning, though they were fewer in number and noticeably less expensive than those received by the "real" children in the families. What child is not crestfallen when the glittering gift wrap is torn away only to reveal three sets of Fruit of the Loom undershorts and T-shirts and a half-dozen pairs of white socks?

But that Christmas, I knew there would be no gifts for me under the tree. I don't recall if we even *had* a tree that year. I knew that if I wanted Christmas gifts, I would have to buy them myself. And that meant finding the money to do so.

I most often "found" money in the top drawer of my father's dresser, into which he emptied wads of bills that were damp from having lain on the bar of the Kenwood Tavern in tiny puddles of condensation left by bottles of Budweiser beer. I told myself I was no mere thief. I rarely took money for purely recreational purposes. No, I stole money almost exclusively for food, often having to scrounge for change in my father's pockets or the seams of the living room furniture to put together enough cash for a greasy burger, fries, and a Coke at Gino Marchetti's on Route 13. I did this only when there was no Campbell's Cream of Chicken soup in the house, which I heated, undiluted, and served over Minute Rice to make a poor man's chicken à la king, or no English muffins to toast and slather with Ragù spaghetti sauce and a slice of American cheese to make "pizza."

My father's bedroom was usually dark. He often retreated there to drink, and he kept the curtains drawn, creating a cave-like refuge that smelled faintly of sweat, stale beer, and cigarette smoke. The inside of his dresser drawers, however, still retained a distinct and not unpleasant aroma of the dark wood from which they were made–cherry, maybe, or mahogany. I could imagine there were still pockets of air within them from when they had occupied a row house in Brooklyn, New York, from which my parents had moved in the first year of the Eisenhower Administration, seeking a new life in a utopian suburban development in Northeast Philadelphia.

On this occasion, I struck pay dirt. Nestled in a corner of the fragrant top drawer was a fat roll from which I peeled a five- or ten-dollar bill. I don't recall which. A five would have gotten me what I wanted: two model car kits at $1.49 apiece, two cans of spray paint, a tube of glue, some candy. A ten would have been extravagant. Anything more than that, a twenty or a fifty, was encountered so rarely as to seem like foreign currency. In any event, such large denominations were almost certain to be missed.

I remember little of my mile-long journey to the "Shop-A-Rama," as our then-revolutionary open-air mall was called. I would have walked down our street, Garden Lane, past my elementary school, John Fitch (named for the unsung inventor of the steamboat, for which the credit went to Robert Fulton), then along Farmbrook Drive to Kenwood Drive, each of which circled a distinct neighborhood of nearly identical homes like a bracelet.

The temperature was moderate for late December; it would not be a white Christmas. I don't recall encountering even a single other person on my journey. No Christmas greetings were exchanged, and I was oblivious to whatever holiday festivities and preparations might have been going on behind the closed front doors of the homes I passed. I suppose I was focused on what model cars I would select–a sleek '65 Chevy Impala SS coupe? A Pontiac GTO? What color paint would I choose? Candy apple red for the GTO, surely. Silver or gold metal-flake for the Chevy? With ten dollars I'd even have enough money left over to buy a package of the flocked velvet cloth on adhesive backing designed to provide realistic upholstery to the 1/24 scale-model interiors of the cars.

It was twilight as I reached the portion of Kenwood Drive that curved to the right toward the Shop-A-Rama. I braced myself to battle the last-minute shoppers I would find in the basement of the Woolworth's five-and-dime, hoping that the selection of car kits would not be picked over and I could find the models I wanted.

But as I rounded the bend and the mall came into view, I was greeted by an unexpected sight. The parking lot was not jammed but empty, save for one lonely, seemingly abandoned vehicle. Colorful lights twinkled on the low, flat-roofed, glass-fronted shops, and the public address system quietly played a wordless Christmas carol, but not a single shopper was in sight and the tune echoed hauntingly off the deserted storefronts. The mall had closed early for Christmas Eve, sending employees home to spend the evening with their families–assembling bicycles, wrapping gifts, trimming trees. It was like a scene from *The Twilight Zone*, the one in which Anne Francis plays a solitary shopper who finds herself in a deserted department store, only to learn at the end of the half-hour script that she was a mannequin returning from a month-long "holiday" in the world of the living.

I stood rooted to the spot like an explorer who crests what he thinks is the final peak in a mountain range, only to find himself faced with an impassable abyss. There was no point in making my way across the vast tundra of the parking lot; I knew there was not a chance that the five-and-dime was somehow exempt from closing early.

After so many years, it is impossible to fully recapture the weight of that moment, the crushing sense of powerlessness and defeat, the misplaced hope that with pluck and cunning I could single-handedly rescue Christmas for myself, that there would be a happy ending to this or any Yuletide tale. I don't remember how long I stood there or what I was thinking on the solitary walk home in the dark. I don't recall if I felt more sad or angry. My best guess is that I was simply numb, stunned in the same way I was when the juvenile court abruptly removed me from my first foster family–the good one–the day after denying their custody petition, as if we all had done something wrong and needed to be punished. I do know that no one showed up at home until well into the next afternoon, Christmas day. And I am certain I returned the stolen money to its place in my father's dresser and prayed for absolution at confession the next Saturday, thinking that perhaps I had gotten exactly what I had deserved.

I realize this epic rebuke of the Christmas spirit is a lot to lay at my father's feet. I was fourteen, for God's sake, and had already been through a lot. I had spent *many* evenings home alone after my mother's death. My father often worked nights or spent the evenings with one of a number of widowed women, whom he charmed until he lapsed into his bad habits and they dumped him. For the most part, I didn't mind the solitude. In fact, in many ways I *preferred* it. I'd do my homework, spend time sketching futuristic cars, and watch "grown-up" movies on TV I might otherwise not been allowed to see: *An Affair to Remember, Bonjour Tristesse, Sweet Bird of Youth.*

For this event to have been so memorable to me, something more had to have been going on, something much, much bigger than simply waking up in an empty house on what many people think of as the most wonderful day of the year. I know now that I realized on that day that I was truly alone–not just at home on Christmas but alone in the world. Nobody was looking out for me–not my father, not my siblings, not some anonymous minion in a bureaucratic institution charged with child welfare. Being smart enough and wily enough to look out for myself was no guarantee there would be a happy ending. It's something most people eventually learn, though generally at a much later age. And the lesson was much more brutal because it came at Christmas.

So just what is it that I have learned from this ghost of Christmas past?

I have been "home alone" nearly every Christmas of my adult life. I had a romantic partner on only one Christmas, in 1972, and even that was a disappointment–we broke up six weeks later. Although I remain close to my sister, we have long been separated by hundreds if not thousands of miles and I refuse to deal with the madness of the holiday crush at the airport simply to avoid being alone on Christmas morning. Through the years, I have tried to make the best of my Grinch-like attitude. In the mid-1970s, my habit was to work on Christmas Day as a reporter for the *Orlando Sentinel*, earning double time for what was usually a slow news day–a scheme that backfired spectacularly in 1975, when I walked into a newsroom abuzz about a quadruple murder in a local furniture store on Christmas Eve. In 1978 and 1979, I spent Christmas Eve answering calls overnight at the office of the Samaritans of Rhode Island, a crisis line I helped establish while working at Brown University. One year, I tried to get into the holiday spirit by buying Christmas gifts for the wife and infant son of a man I was sleeping with, which had predictably mixed results. But in general, I have simply ignored the holiday.

In December 2010, I had been living in California for six months. I had lost my job at the height of the Great Recession and after two years of fruitless job-hunting in Washington, DC, I had accepted a friend's offer to retire to his rarely used vacation home in the San Bernardino National Forest. At an altitude of 6,100 feet, a white Christmas was virtually guaranteed, and that year was no exception. One night as the holiday approached, I was sitting at my computer working on a web site I was designing for an author I knew, when I heard a knock at my front door followed by what was unmistakably a Christmas carol. Soft, colorful lights glowed though the curtained window over the kitchen sink.

I panicked! If I opened the door, I likely would come face-to-face with an amateur band of carolers and be forced to smile though some off-key acapella rendition of "Silent Night" or worse, "The Twelve Effing Days of Christmas!" When the song was over, they would expect something. A tip of some sort. A contribution to their high school choir or a donation to a local charity.

I immediately shut down my computer, with its huge, brightly lit high-resolution display. Then I doused the lights in the kitchen and living room and scuttled across the floor to my already darkened bedroom. From that distance, I heard another knock at the door. Another carol. I held my breath and waited for them to leave.

Ten or fifteen minutes later, my cell phone rang. Caller ID indicated that it was one of two women I had met while walking my dog, Bandit–the only two neighbors I knew. When I answered, she told me to go to my front door and open it.

"What? Why?"

"Just go, Andrew."

Outside the door, in a spot cleared of snow, was a small artificial Christmas tree, decorated with tiny ornaments and strung with twinkle lights, now dark. An electrical cord was uncoiled at its base. The two women, one of their sons, and his girlfriend had brought the tree and some sort of portable power source to my door, plugged it in, and started singing. And I, like a cockroach surprised in the kitchen or a gay man in the glare of the lights at last call had scurried into the darkness to hide.

I was mortified!

Still on the phone, I burst into tears... and hysterical, hyena-like laughter.

"I'm sorry," I said. "I am sooo sorry!"

"What is *wrong* with you?"

What, indeed?

I don't think my friend was mad, but I had the feeling she was, at best, confused and disappointed in me. Why on earth had I, at my age, allowed the memory of a Christmas past to spoil the incredibly generous gesture of my new friends to include me in their holiday celebrations? I don't know.

Unlike Ebenezer Scrooge, I didn't have an epiphany that night. I just felt foolish. I didn't rush out and buy a Christmas goose for a disabled child's family, though I will admit to regularly buying one or more of those $10 bags of food for the less fortunate at Thanksgiving or Christmas.

I no longer get upset at the absence of presents. As to the specific events of Christmas 1965, it was just as well that the stores were closed and I didn't get those model car kits after all. Within a couple of years, my father, in a drunken rage, upended a bureau on which I had displayed every model car I had ever built, smashing them to smithereens. It's the kind of ending O. Henry might have written... had he been very, very twisted.

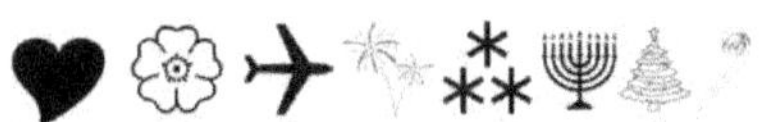

Selected Poetry

Sarah White

MIDNIGHT BLUE

I won't have another bitter December
Starless nights and Old Saint Nick love letters
dragging my innocent essence back to you.
No more turning left on James Street at the stroke midnight
off Woolner Avenue.
No more illicit mistletoes moments blanketed in unholy air
that's midnight blue.
Only blinking lights, peppermint candy, stringing garland and
drawing hearts on frosted windows
And Hanging mom's favorite candy canes.
Those frozen Christmas twelve-o-clock memories still remain
I wanted more than your December nights
You wanted to inflict that midnight pain.
I wanted that shimmering ring in vow of our daylight flame
You wanted more of the same; watched me as I chased your
last name.
I'll never be 19 those winter nights with anyone but you
Dancing in the Christmas tree's light, painted tippy toes, no
shoes
Loving you in a lavender haze with glitter gold hues
You loved me with sinister eyes toning midnight blue.
Warm vanilla scent, the perfumed mascot of our witching
hour
Freeing our lips from inhibitions like blooming Poinsettia
flowers
Like clockwork you reminiscent how my crimson lace is
detained by you
You bring it out every winter and by January it's midnight blue

Left me so lifeless. Paralyzed by consequences. Emotional bruises are tattoos.
You left me so icy, sitting in hurt, your intent was midnight blue.
I buried the scarlet lace I left at your mom's place and every December you resurrect it.
Christmas was believing the fault in our stars with my shaking hand in your right coat pocket
Balmy cuddles on a worn-in couch, cold midnight breeze creeps in as the TV's turned down low
Your selfish, masterminded intentions of taking advantage down below
Frost bites from midnight takes control of my yuletide soul
You iced our whole city over like some nonchalant maleficent pro.
Breathe in, hold deep, breathe out mist of midnight blue fog
The mirror ball of my essence no longer reflects off broken versions of you
Now healing. Breathing. Wide awake, well past the hours of Midnight Blue.

Never Have I Ever

Walking to the small town bar in the highest heels I own.
Air is misty and frigid cold.
On the cheap rooftop bars I pass there are cascading icicles.
Moon is shining an incandescent glow on the familiar path I stroll.
The stars are ever clear. Frosted breath, wind in my hair.
Typical last night of the year.
Door opens, how was I to know?
I'd be dead stopped in my tracks, frozen at the threshold.
Not by the outside frosty air, but by the air you breathe.
You sat at the far end of the bar with tricks up your rolled up sleeves.
Never have I ever been attracted to a she.
The intensity of this attraction across the room and my wide eye gaze,
The complexity of her masculinity and femininity consumes me in a enamored haze.
I'm going through a list in my mind of what could be her name.
I wish to know what's it like to be only what's hers, the spirited cup pressed against her lips.
Pinned thoughts of past male lovers are going down like sinking ships.
Life before her presence and this moment seems so dishonest.
How is this classic News Year Eve I was promised?
Oh how I wish I can write my name on her.
Wanting her isn't enough.
She interlaces desire through our locked eyes as the surrounding James Dean's scuff.

She trips over party-goers and lovers as she make her way through the crowd.
I trip on words to say and what to do with my hands, blurring out all sound.
Everything I've known about lust and magnetic fields changes right now.
"Maddie," she flirts.
"Carrie," I say, inelegantly sipping on my chintzy rosé.
An accidental push brings her even closer to my lips.
Her maroon cocktail splashes onto me, staining my lustrous white sequins.
I know this stain is the moment where my life truly begins.
There's an erogenous fever neither of us can no longer stand.
She reaches out.
Oh goddamn, my inhibitions fit into the palm of her tepid hand.
Never have I ever felt a hand like this from another.
Blood rushes to my cheeks turning them some foreign shade of scarlet.
Leading me hand in hand to the bathroom like we're two starlets on the red carpet.
There's now complex tension ricocheting in this bar and she started it
Sealing my fate, the door shuts and the lock quietly clicks.
Never have I ever had a moment like this.
Lifting me up from my skirt onto the sink counter.
She is gorgeous, so suave, so self-assured.
Turning on my raging lust, running me like water.
Never have I ever needed anything more.
She takes a berg of ice from that very glass I was once jealous of.
Sensually runs the ice down the center of my chest, memorizing every drop.
I'm bursting inside with intense obsession, lust, and love.
I feel my soul taking its first breath.

Unhurried, she's growing on me like ivy. I can't resist. I am covered in her.
Pressing her yielding lips on my sweating neck, tangling our fingers together.
Grazing her every curve, counting every freckle on her exposed breast by her heart.
Her seductive poised touch brings out a bejeweled mark on my every part.
Trembling and moaning from intimacy, ecstasy, and sexual truth.
She reaches behind me and turns on the faucet to the clean the stain.
"No," I flick her hand away.
"I never want to be clean from you."
Fairytales kill for moments like this we stole.
Respiring what's left of this year with her with nothing to lose, no cards to fold.
Please don't tell me we're on begged and barrowed time.
I'm finally breathing in and exhaling a truth that's pure and mine.
New Years Eve was a love letter placed right into our intertwined hands.
The iridescent stars, unfinished encounters, and spilled cocktails all seem so planned.
5… 4… 3… 2…1. Euphoric celebration is heard from strangers on the other side of the door.
Happy New Year.
Happy new queer.

About the Authors

K.S. Trenten

K.S. Trenten lives in the South Bay area with her husband, two cats, and a crowd of characters in her head; all shouting for attention. Follow K.S. Trenten, locate her published works, or read free samples at…

Facebook

http://www://facebook.com/rhodrymavelyne/

Twitter

https://twitter.com/rhodrymavelyne

Goodreads

https://www.goodreads.com/author/show/14876500.K_S_Trenten

Amazon Author Page

http://www.amazon.com/author/kstrenten

Nine Star Press Author Page

https://ninestarpress.com/authors/k-s-trenten/

The Cauldron of Eternal Inspiration

http://www://inspirationcauldron.wordpress.com

Pat Henshaw

Pat Henshaw has led an interesting life starting as a theatrical costumer, then moving to newspaper editor, arts reviewer, and book columnist. In addition to newspapers, she worked as a publicist and an English composition instructor. Her most challenging roles have been as a wife, a mother to two brilliant daughters, and grandma to twins.

Although she was born in Nebraska, she has lived on all three U.S. coasts: in Texas, in Northern Virginia, and in California. She has also traveled extensively around the world, on a trip down the Nile, riding an elephant in Thailand, and touring Europe. After she retired, she fulfilled a lifelong dream to become an author. Through all her life experiences, she still maintains: ***Every day is a good day for romance***.

R.L. Merrill

R.L. Merrill brings you stories of Hope, Love, and Rock 'n' Roll featuring quirky and relatable characters. Whether she's writing contemporary, paranormal, or supernatural, she loves to give readers a shiver with compelling stories that will stay with you long after. You can find her connecting with readers on social media, advocating for America's youth, raising two brilliant teenagers, writing horror-infused music reviews for HorrorAddicts.net, trying desperately to get that back piece finished in the tattoo chair, or headbanging at a rock show near her home in the San Francisco Bay Area! Stay tuned for more Rock 'n' Romance.

Liz Faraim

Liz Fariam has a full plate between balancing a day job, parenting, writing, and finding some semblance of a social life. In past lives, she has been a soldier, a bartender, a shoe salesperson, an assistant museum curator, and even a driving instructor. She focuses her writing on strong, queer, female leads who don't back down. Liz transplanted to California from New York over thirty years ago, and now lives in the East Bay Area. She enjoys exploring nature with her wife and son.

Richard May

Richard May writes Gay fiction. His work has appeared in numerous literary journals, story anthologies, and his collections *Ginger Snaps: Photos & Stories of Redheaded Queer People, Inhuman Beings,* and *Gay All Year: Twelve Stories.* He is a member of the18th Street Writers and the Bay Area Queer Writers Association. Rick organizes the Odd Mondays and Perfectly Queer reading series. He lives in San Francisco.

Vincent Traughber Meis

Vincent Traughber Meis worked for many years as an English as a Second Language (ESL) teacher in the San Francisco Bay Area, Spain, Saudi Arabia and Mexico, publishing many academic articles in his field. He published travel articles, poems, and book reviews in publications such as, *The Advocate, LA Weekly, In Style,* and *Our World* in the 1980s and 1990s. Seven of his eight published novels are set at least partially in foreign countries, and his book of short stories focuses on countries around the world. Several of his novels have won Rainbow Awards and two of his novels, including *First Born Sons,* were awarded Reader Views Silver Awards. He has published short stories in a number of collections and has achieved Finalist status in a few short fiction contests. He lives in San Leandro, California and Puerto Vallarta, Mexico.

M.D. Neu

Growing up in an accepting family author M.D. Neu always wondered why there were never stories reflecting our diverse queer society. Surrounded by characters that only mirrored heterosexual society, he decided to change that and began writing, wanting to tell epic stories that reflect our varied world. Over the years, Neu has written several Urban Fantasy, Science Fiction, and Paranormal works. His Science Fiction novels *A New World-Contact* and *Conviction* won the 2018-2019 International Rainbow Awards: Best Gay Alternative Universe/Reality & Sci-Fi / Futuristic books. Recently, his novella *T.A.D.-The Angel of Death* won the 2020-2021 International Rainbow Awards: Best Gay Alternative Universe/Reality and was one of the Runner Ups for Best Gay Book. Neu's debut novel, *The Calling,* was featured in the *San Jose Mercury News* (January 2018) garnering him national recognition. When not writing M.D. Neu works for a non-profit in Silicon Valley and travels with his husband of twenty-plus years.

Kelliane Parker

Kelliane Parker is a queer, Latinx Bay Area poet and the author of, *Down the Foggy Streets of My Mind*, from Nomadic Press. Her work focuses on healing from trauma and living with Dissociative Identity Disorder. She very proud to be a new member of the Bay Area Queer Writers Association, (BAQWA). Kelliane has been featured in numerous anthologies including the recent Lawrence Ferlinghetti tribute anthology, *Light on the Walls of Life*, edited by Bobby Coleman. You can find her performing all over the Bay Area and Zoomlandia.

Allison Fradkin

Allison Fradkin (she/her) has a gay old time applying her Women's & Gender Studies education to the creation of satirically scintillating prose, poetry, and plays that (sur)pass the Bechdel Test and enlist their characters in a caricature of the idiocies and intricacies of insidious isms. She has contributed to *Sapphic Writers Collective, Emblazoned Soul Literary Review, Pastel Serenity, ImageOutWrite, Synkroniciti, Voyage, Chaotic Merge, Femme Problems, Slamming Bricks, Rejoinder, The Bard Review, Dirty Mouth, Loud and Queer, Continue the Voice, New Plains Review*, and *Proud of Rust and Glass: A Midwest Pride Anthology*. Allison's auxiliary activities include vintage shopping, volunteering, and tending to her thespian tendencies.

Wayne Goodman

Wayne Goodman has lived in the San Francisco Bay Area most of his life (with too many cats). Goodman hosts Queer Words Podcast, conversations with queer-identified authors about their works and lives. When not writing or recording, he enjoys playing Gilded Age parlor music on the piano, with an emphasis on women, gay, and Black composers.

Alexandra Caluen

Alexandra Caluen lives in a small purple house with her husband, a bottle of Laphroaig, a lot of books, and nine pairs of ballroom shoes. She is the author of over fifty contemporary romance novels and novellas featuring creative, diverse characters.

Connect with Alexandra:

Queeromance Ink
Alexandra Caluen
Instagram
@the.l.a.stories
Blog
http://thelastories.com

Andrew Beierle

Andrew W. M. Beierle is the author of *The Winter of Our Discothèque* (Kensington, 2002), winner of a 2003 Lambda Literary Award, and *First Person Plural* (Kensington, 2007), a finalist for the 2007 men's fiction Lammy. His short fiction has been published in the Harrington Gay Men's Fiction Quarterly and *Rebel Yell: Stories by Contemporary Southern Gay Authors* (Harrington Park Press, 2001). His personal essays have appeared in *Catamaran,* a quarterly journal of literature and art published in Santa Cruz. He lives on the Central Coast of California with his dog, Bandit.

Sarah White

Hanging out in her thirties, Sarah is a bisexual, born and raised Bay Area native. Sarah writes queer culture and queer historical articles for a national LGBTQ magazine, is an LGBTQ activist, and a youth crisis counselor for the Trevor Project. "Liking the wine and not the label" (*Schitt's Creek* reference) is Sarah's favorite part of being bisexual because she is living proof that love and attraction is not binary, it is continuous, untamed, and pure. Sarah writes her poetry based on her real life experiences of thriving and failing at love as a bisexual woman in the 21st Century. Sarah would like to thank BAQWA for this humbling opportunity to showcase her writing and provide a platform to connect with other queer people leaving their rainbow mark on the world by just breathing in and breathing out their truth.

All proceeds from this limited-time anthology will be donated to the Rainbow Community Center in Concord, California.

www.ingramcontent.com/pod-product-compliance
Lightning Source LLC
Chambersburg PA
CBHW070355200726
48294CB00003B/917
9781959257035